THIS HOUSE
IS NOT
FOR SALE

ALSO BY E. C. OSONDU

Voice of America

THIS HOUSE
IS NOT
FOR SALE

E. C. Osondu

GRANTA

Granta Publications, 12 Addison Avenue, London W11 4QR

First published in Great Britain by Granta Books, 2015
First published in the United States by HarperCollins Publishers,
New York, 2015

A CIP catalogue record for this book
is available from the British Library.

1 3 5 7 9 10 8 6 4 2

ISBN 978 1 84708 182 7 (hardback)
ISBN 978 1 84708 818 5 (ebook)

Offset by M Rules

Printed and bound by CPI Group (UK) Ltd, Croydon, CR0 4YY

www.grantabooks.com

MIX
Paper from
responsible sources
FSC
www.fsc.org   FSC® C020471

In loving memory of my dearly beloved sister,
Felicia Maria Ezediuno Nwanze

THIS HOUSE
IS NOT
FOR SALE

HOW THE HOUSE CAME TO BE

When we asked Grandpa how the house we all called the Family House came into existence, this was the story he told us.

A long, long time ago, before anybody alive today was born, a brave ancestor of ours who was also a respected and feared juju man woke up one day and told his family, friends, and neighbors that he had a dream. In the dream he saw a crown being placed on his head. He interpreted this dream as signifying that he was going to be crowned a king soon.

As was the custom in those days, a new king had to be crowned by a reigning king who would also hand him a scepter of office. This should not have been a problem but for a minor incident that had occurred in the palace many,

many years ago, before even those who were telling this story were born. You see, our ancestors had a bit of history with the palace.

We were told that my people once lived under the hegemony of an oppressive king in the distant past. Because they spoke a different language, and had two diagonal scarifications on each cheek, not much respect was accorded them. Not much was expected from them, either, other than the occasional payment of tributes to the king. They lived on the fringes of the society. They were neither full citizens nor bondsmen.

When a hunter among these ancestors of the family killed a wild boar he was expected to send the choicest part of the kill to the king.

When a girl child was born to them and it was seen by all eyes that she was indeed fair on the eyes and pretty, everyone began to refer to her as the king's prospective wife. When she grew up she would be taken to the palace so that the king would peek at her through a peephole. If she caught his fancy and he liked what he saw, she became one of his wives. If he didn't like her, she could then be married to someone else. It was said that some women who were pregnant in those days would eat bitter leaves, chew bitter kola nuts, and drink bitter fluids, putting themselves through all kinds of painful and bitter ordeals in order to ensure that their female offspring were born ugly.

The king had also mandated that the menfolk of the family should take part in the building of a large moat that was conceived to go round the kingdom like the Great Wall of China. This was going to be the king's landmark achievement. It was in the nature of kings to build something that they would be remembered by. In later years court oral historians could then intone that during the reign of so and so king a great wall was erected around the kingdom to protect his subjects from invasion. To build a moat, mud was needed, and this mud had to be kneaded. This was a hard task. The digging out of the mud from a wide and deep hole and the fetching of water to knead it and the ferrying of the mud on baskets on the head. A rebellious ancestor complained about this humiliating task of mud kneading and moat building and had suggested they knead the mud with palm oil instead. This was done.

The next morning, the king's palace was overrun by soldier ants.

It was important that a king should be feared by his subjects as such, any form of or hint of rebellion must be punished and crushed. This king was no different, he knew this rule of kingship and decided to teach these ancestors a lesson that they will never forget.

The king was determined to kill my ancestors. They fled on foot and would have settled in a town close to where they eventually settled but they were repulsed by the sight of *pregnant men*. This mystery would be later explained. The men were not really pregnant. Their large protruding bellies were a result of consuming lots of palm wine.

It was to this palace that this ancestor wanted to return in order to be crowned king and to be handed a scepter of office.

When this ancestor was getting ready to go on the trip he invited some of his brothers and neighbors to come along with him, but they refused. They all knew that the unleashing of the soldier ants incident had not been forgiven or forgotten. Palaces tend to have a long memory. Yet this ancestor insisted that some people should come along with him. He knew that he needed to be crowned in the presence of witnesses. He eventually persuaded two of his friends to go with him after he had promised them official positions when he became king.

As expected, immediately they announced their presence, they were arrested and detained. The next morning one of them was brought out to the king's courtyard. In the words of the king it was important to teach those who thought they could question royal authority a lesson they would never forget. The king was incensed for two reasons. He could tell from the diagonal tribal scarifications on the faces of these men, one of whom wanted to be crowned king, that they were the same people who had refused to build the moat and had unleashed the soldier ants that overran the palace. And now they also wanted to be crowned king. Unless this was dealt with ruthlessly, who knew what other form of rebellion they could incite his loyal subjects into committing? All the men, women, and children in the kingdom were assembled to witness this interesting spectacle. The king gave an order for the two men to be tied up. The king ordered that the first man be beheaded. It was done.

The next day the second man also had his head cut off. It was now my ancestor's turn. He had spent the entire period of his detention red eyed and head bowed in sorrow over the loss of his friends. His own safety did not concern him that much. He was the one who had persuaded his late friends to come along with him on the journey. It was for this fact alone that he felt some regret.

As he was tied up and the sword unsheathed from the scabbard to chop off his head as the king had ordered, a millipede crawled out from his thick mane of hair and emerged from the center of his head. It was dark brown.

"Halt," the king ordered his executioner.

He was a king, he had seen many things, but he also knew and respected strong juju. This was no mere mortal. The millipede was a sign that this man was a strong juju man. The king's attitude changed.

"Untie the man," the king commanded.

"Prepare him good food. Dress him in the best clothes and bring him into my presence tomorrow."

It was done.

When the ancestor was brought to the king's presence the next day, the king sent all his courtiers away and sat alone with my ancestor. My ancestor looked the king in the eye and said to him, "I know what keeps you awake at night. You are worried that you will die young like your father and your great-grandfather and all your ancestors who have been kings before you."

The king looked at my ancestor and nodded humbly.

"I will make you an amulet that will make you live to a ripe old age. You must go into the forest yourself and gather me some wild vines," my ancestor said to the king.

"I have thousands of slaves and servants that can do it, I

will send one of them or even a dozen of them to pluck you this vine," the king said.

"Yes, I know, but you must pick the wild vine yourself. It is important that you do this yourself because only you can extend your own life. No other hand can extend your life for you."

So the king went into the forest and came back with the wild vine. My ancestor plucked the leaves off the vine and twisted the vine into a twine and hung it to dry on a rafter by the fireplace. Three days later he summoned the king and asked the king to bring down the now-dry twisted vine. The king did.

"Twist it and see if you can break it in two."

The king twisted it, and the vine broke in two without much effort on the king's part.

"You must go into the forest once again and bring me the same vine," he told the king. Once again, the king complained but went to the forest and got the vines. This time, my ancestor ordered that the vine was to be hung up in the rafters and the fires must be kept burning at low heat for seven days. After seven days the vine was given to the king to break in two, but no matter how much he tried he could not break it in two. My ancestor now pounded the dry creeping vine in a mortar and used it to prepare a longevity talisman for the king that was to be worn around the neck. He also told the king.

"From now going forward, decree that when you or any of your descendants dies, they be buried in an upright position while seated on their royal stool. Only commoners deserve to be buried on their backs, lying down. When you get to the world beyond, you'll discover there are also hierarchies as we have here on earth, there are levels in the next world, you know. Over there, you'll also be counted among the royalty and accorded the deference and respect you deserve." The king was delighted by this idea of reigning among the living and the dead and decreed that this would be the manner in which all kings, including him, would be buried from then on.

"How do I repay you?" the king asked.

"You should grant me my original request. Crown me king."

"There cannot be two kings in the land," the king said. "Here's what I'll do. I will give you a large parcel of land somewhere in the outskirts, and money and men to start life afresh. I will also build you a mansion where you will live. A mansion that befits a strong juju man like you."

And that was how we acquired the land on which the Family House was built. The king also built this ancestor a mansion, but it was built out of mud. Many years later the son of the king was sent to visit the king of Portugal. When he came back, he described the kind of houses he saw in Portugal. As a final gift the king, who had now lived to a ripe old age, decided to build the Family House in the Portuguese architectural style for my ancestor. What my ancestor did not know was that the king had built him the house in order to keep an eye on him. He had instructed his soldiers to kill my ancestor if for any reason the king did not live to a ripe old age. This was how the Family House came to be.

NDOZO

We were all woken up one morning by shouts of thief! thief! We were summoned to the large sitting room, the parlor. One of the women who lived in the house was kneeling down on the floor and was crying. Her name was Ndozo. She was one among the many women that sold for Grandpa in the market. She also had a little son whose nose was always snotty and who wore three aluminum crucifixes tied on a string around his neck and a talisman around the waist. They said she had been stealing from the money made from sales. She was one of the trusted ones. She was one of those that counted the money at the end of each day. She was accused of helping herself to some of the money.

"How long have you been stealing from the sales money?" one of the older men living in the house asked her.

Her interrogator's name was Sibe-Sibe. He had lived in the house for so long that no one remembered what he was exactly. He occupied that unclear borderland between servant and freeborn. All the servants feared him. Grandpa respected and trusted him.

"Not for such a long time," she said.

"One month? One year? Three months? Just tell us how long?"

"I don't remember how long," she said. "It is the devil. I promise never to do it again."

"We will show how we deal with thieves in the Family House."

Someone grabbed a Tiger razor blade from its packet and began to scrape off her hair. There was no pretense or attempt at giving her a proper haircut, the shoddier the job, the better, this haircut was intended to humiliate, not beautify. Soon most of her hair was on the floor though there were still small tufts of hair on some parts of her scalp. Some parts of her scalp were bleeding where the blade had nicked her skin.

They stripped her of her clothes, leaving only her under-skirt made of different-colored cotton fabric. They made a necklace out of snail shells and strung it around her neck. She was given two empty milk cans and told to start clapping them together like cymbals. We were told to follow her as she was forced to walk out of the house half-naked.

"I will never steal again. It was the devil. I don't know why I did. This is my family. I have no other family. Please, I promise not to steal again."

But Grandpa wanted to use her to set an example. He said that it was important that we saw how thieves were treated so that we would never be tempted to steal in our lives.

As she was led down the steps out into the streets the men told her to sing. One of the men was holding a long *koboko* horse whip and would mockingly act as if he were going to whip her, at which she'd jump and the snail shells would make a mild rattling sound. She clapped the empty milk cans together and began to walk down the street as we followed her. We were told to make booing noises and jeer at her as we walked behind her. As soon as we left the house because it was still early morning, we passed by people bringing out their wares and women frying *akara*. They would pause in their morning activity and turn to us and she would be made to stand before them as she clapped the empty milk tins together and sing and we ululated behind her.

"What did you do?" they'd ask, even though they already knew from seeing her shaved head and the snail shell mock necklace around her neck.

"I stole."

"And what did you steal?"

"I stole money from the sales box."

"And what did you do with the money?"

"It was the devil that made me do it."

"Will you ever steal again?" they'd ask her.

"No, I will never steal again," she would say.

"Now do your song and dance for us again. It is a good song, we like hearing it."

She would dance and clap her empty milk cans together as she sang:

Thief, thief, jankoriko
Ajibole ole

We moved from the Family House through different streets and warrens and side streets. At some point she said she was thirsty because the sun was out and burning but she was immediately told to shut her mouth. She said she wanted to urinate but she was told to pee on herself. She said her throat was hurting and that she was losing her voice, but they asked if she would have stopped stealing if she hadn't been caught.

"It was the devil that made me do it," she said.

We were getting tired too, but still we walked and walked a bit more and she stopped and sang and stopped and sang and people asked her what she had done.

When we got back home she was told to go and kneel in the same corner where she had been kneeling when we woke up. She was not allowed to touch her son.

"You see how thieves are treated in the Family House?" we were asked.

"That is exactly what will happen to anyone who steals in this house, including my own children and grandchildren."

The next morning when we woke up, Ndozo had vanished, leaving her infant son behind.

There were lots of stories about her disappearance. Some said she had been so consumed by shame, she had gone and thrown herself into the lagoon. Others said she had run back to her parents. Nobody could recall who her parents were. She was one of those that had come to live in the house in exchange for some money owed Grandpa until the money was paid back, then she could return to her family. But it was said that whoever borrowed from Grandpa was never in a position to repay because he jinxed them and many of them remained in the house and had children who also became a part of the Family House, helping around the house until they became old enough to go and start selling in the store.

It was said that before Ndozo left the house she had placed a curse on the house, saying that just as she had been put to shame that the house and its inhabitants would eventually be humiliated and come to shame.

Someone said that Grandpa had whispered that she was not going to be missed and that she had done a good thing by leaving her son behind.

Years later, a car parked in front of the Family House and a plump woman stepped out. She was dressed expensively. She shielded her eyes as she looked at the house, as if she needed to reassure herself that this was indeed her destination. She walked through the gate and entered the compound. It was

Ndozo. She greeted and asked for Grandpa. She excused herself and went back to the car. The driver began to carry things into the house. Plastic containers and clothes. She said she had come to take her son back with her. She was now a big trader in plastics in the neighboring country. She said she had been blessed with everything, good fortune and riches; her business had prospered. She had started out as an apprentice, selling plastics to a big trader over there, and because she was good in business, knew how to attract customers, and sell at a profit, all of them skills she had acquired from living in the Family House, she had made the business of her boss grow. She said that all she was today she owed to her time selling for Grandpa. Her boss soon opened a shop of her own for her and the shop had really grown in size. She was now a big distributor of plastics. She even had people selling for her. She was sorry for that theft of a long time ago but she was also happy that something good had come out of it. Here she was today, prosperous and independent. She had people selling for her and she would be disappointed if they stole from her. She was here to make restitution. She had found love, she had met a man who loved her and they were married, but she had been unable to conceive. People said that a woman must choose between the kind of wealth that can be counted, such as money and landed property and cars, and the type that cannot be counted, for you can count the number of cattle that you have but you do not count your children. Where was her son? she asked. She wanted to see him and touch him with her hands. In all the years that had gone by there had not been a day that his face and thoughts of him had left her mind.

There was silence. They let her words sink in, then they came at her like angry wasps.

"And you want us to believe your story. Your story is too sweet to be true."

"You have been stealing from the money box in the store before you were caught."

"You must have been sending all the money to your partners in the neighboring country who must have invested it for you."

"You were selling plastics, indeed. Don't we have plastic sellers here, how many of them have become rich, if what you claim is true."

"And you think you can just come back here and take your son back. Suppose we tell you that he fell sick and died, what then?"

She began to cry, and all of a sudden she was the old Ndozo. Her expensive clothes began to look like a masquerade costume. She said she knew it in her soul that her son was still alive. She said they should compute all the money and interest of the money she took from the money box all those years ago and she would pay it back.

She said she was ready to give all she owned to the family if only she could be allowed to leave with her son.

"And all the salt, all the pepper, all the soap, all the medicines, and all the clothes the boy had worn these years, was she ready to pay for them too?"

She pleaded with them to tell her what it was going to cost her.

"Suppose we tell you that the boy is dead. That after you left for days the boy refused to eat or drink. He kept pointing at the road, asking for his mother. Asking when she would return to cuddle the way he was used to being cuddled at night. He was told that his mother would soon be back. He cried even more and as he cried his body became hot and he began running a fever and then fainted. He was rushed to the hospital but the doctor said it was too late, his heart was already broken; the doctor said he had never seen a heart that broken in one so young."

"I know in my heart, the way only a mother can know, that my son is still alive, I can hear his heart beating."

"How can you call yourself a mother when you abandoned him when he most needed a mother's warmth, the joy of hearing you call his name, telling him that the evening meal is ready and he leaves his playmates and comes running toward you, his nose in the air, drinking in the aroma of well-made soup."

"All the years I have been away, I have always thought about him and about this house. I know I did bad and that was why I left. I have always wanted to ask for forgiveness for what I did and show my gratitude. I always thought that this will be a day of joy and reunion and reconciliation."

"So what were you expecting? You were expecting us to roll out the drums for a common thief who stole from the money box and fled to set up her own trading business with money stolen from this house?"

"To worsen matters you also left your own son to die in our hands."

At every turn they countered her pleading. They turned on her. They twisted her words. Her voice turned hoarse from begging. Her knees went sore from kneeling on the hard ground. The tears on her face formed a crusty, salty dry rivulet.

Finally she stood up and left.

Here is what we heard. She took all the things she had brought with her to share with people in the Family House. She took them to the Beggars Lane. That night, the king of beggars told all the female beggars to follow her to the Family House. When it was midnight, they all bared their buttocks on the house and began to rain curses on the house. They cursed and prayed for evil to befall us and did not stop until dawn began to whisper gently into the ears of dusk and then they departed.

Ndozo left for her trading post along the border and never returned. Her son was still alive but he grew up never knowing who his mother was.

IBE

My cousin Ibegbunemkaotitojialimchi, meaning "O save me from my enemies so I can live to the evening of my days on this good earth," or Ibe for short, was staying in the Family House that summer too. Unlike some of us who would be going back to our homes after the long summer holidays before school reopened at the end of the rainy season, Ibe and his mom didn't know when they would be returning to their home in the North. He and his mother left the North because his father had married a second wife. Ibe was the same age as me, but he appeared to know more about the ways of the world. He knew many secrets. He claimed he could perform magic tricks. He claimed he could speak many languages, including a smattering of Hindi, Chinese, and some Arabic.

Ibe said if one wanted to beat one's opponent's team in a soccer match then one must go and capture the biggest redheaded *agama* lizard that one could find. *Agama* lizards were abundant, always sunning themselves unconcernedly on cement blocks in the adjoining uncompleted building. Kill the *agama* lizard, Ibe said, and tie a little piece of red cloth around the lizard's neck, drive a pin through the lizard's head and bury it in a hole by your goalpost. According to Ibe, you have effectively *tied* your opponent and no matter how much they tried they could never get the ball past your goal mouth or score a goal against you.

Ibe said it was also possible to padlock an enemy's brain so the person would fail their exams. Here's how—buy a Yeti or Tokoz padlock, unlock the padlock, and simultaneously whisper your enemy's name and the incantation *read and forget, read and forget* seven times, as you lock the padlock and throw the keys away. When your enemy gets into the exam hall, he'll forget all he has read because you have effectively padlocked his brain.

Ibe said the best soccer coaches gave their players tea laced with an intoxicating pill capsule. This way, the players never got tired while playing and had relentless stamina. He said the reason why India never featured in the soccer World Cup was because they had strong magic. In their first and only appearance in the World Cup, according to Ibe, they had scored over a dozen goals against their opponent. Their opponent's goalkeeper later told the sporting press that each time an Indian player shot the ball in his direction, he saw over a dozen soccer balls hurtling toward him and became confused as to which to catch; he inevitably caught the wrong one. Ibe said this was the reason why Indians had moved on to cricket, where it was normal to score a century.

Ibe said if one loved a girl and did not want her to leave you for another boy, then one should mix one's blood with that of the girl in a blood covenant. A blood covenant was easy, he said. Make an incision on the girl's wrist and make an incision on yours with a sharp razor blade, allow a drop of blood from your wrist to drop into the incision on her wrist to mix your blood with hers; both of you should then dip your finger into the mixed blood and touch it to your tongue. After the blood covenant, if the girl attempts to leave you for another boy, she'll lose her mind and go insane. He knew a girl who wandered around the streets in the northern part of the country half-naked, picking up rubbish. Everyone knew it was because she had broken a blood covenant with her boyfriend.

Ibe said if you want to see your girl in your dreams, place her picture under your pillow and call her name seven times before you fall asleep, and she'll most certainly come to you in the dream.

Ibe said that if you wanted to know all life's secrets, all you needed to do was read a book called *The Sixth and Seventh Books of Moses*. The book contained all the secrets of the world, including the secret way to riches. But there was a catch, according to Ibe. The book must be read at midnight by the light of a lone red candle. The candle must not burn out before one finished reading the entire book. If the candle burns out and one has not finished reading the entire book, madness was sure to follow. Ibe claimed he owned the book and had a red candle too, but was waiting a few more years before reading the book and growing very rich.

Ibe said he knew how to make a potion out of leaves and feathers that could protect us from snakebites and scorpion stings, but he was not going to show it to me because, from past experience, each time he used the potion, snakes and scorpions would crawl out of their holes and would begin following him around almost as if they were taunting him to find out if his potion was effective or not.

Ibe said the market in the town where they had lived in the North was a place of wonder and spectacles. He said that magicians and entertainers came to the market and that he and his friends were allowed to go watch them. He said he had once watched as a magician brought out a sharp sword and attempted to run it through his own belly, but the sharp sword was unable to cut through the skin. The magician had then asked for a volunteer from the crowd. A few volunteers had come forward, including Ibe. They tried cutting the man with the sword but the sword would not cut through the skin. Ibe said when he attempted cutting the magician's belly with the sword, the skin felt like steel.

Ibe said that his father worked for the federal government. His father worked for the national telephone service as a telephone operator. His father could not leave his post because he was an important man. He could reach the head of the country through his little finger. He said his father had memorized the entire country's telephone numbers and area codes. He was an important man.

Ibe said that he did not like the girls in this city because they had flat noses. The girls in the northern part of the country were fair skinned and had pointed noses. They were shy but beautiful.

Ibe said he was going to order a talisman from India called *pocketneverdries*. He said if one had the talisman in one's pocket, one will never run out of money to spend, one will always have the correct amount of money down to the smallest change to make all one's purchases.

Ibe said our *suya* here tasted stringy and was completely juiceless because the meat was from old cows, whereas the *suya* in the North was juicy and succulent because it was made from young calves and rams.

Ibe's mom went to the post office every Friday to check if there was a letter from her husband. He was supposed to write and tell her when he was coming to beg Grandfather so she could return to his house. Whenever she returned from the post office empty-handed, as always she would lock herself in her room and would not talk with anyone for a few days.

Ibe said one could make money from hiring out one's services to a beggar as a stickboy. One simply led the beggar by his stick and went with him from door to door shouting *Bambi Allah*. He said he once had a part-time gig as a stickboy. But he also said the beggars over here were all con men: they only pretended to be blind but they were not really blind. He said they applied gum arabic to their eyes to appear blind and washed off the adhesive at night before they prayed.

Ibe said that this our city was a bad city because unlike in the North, where there was a sign saying WELCOME TO THE NORTH. COME AND LIVE IN PEACE, no sign welcomed anyone to this city except for the billboard proclaiming YOU ARE NOW IN THIS CITY. According to Ibe, nobody was welcome here and one was here at one's own risk.

Ibe said the strongest man in the whole world was not Mighty Igor, the wrestler we all watched on World Wide Wrestling every Thursday at 8:00 PM, but a man called Kill-We. Kill-We had a single bone, unlike us mere mortals, who had multiple bones. He could pull a stationary tractor trailer with one hand. As a result of his special powers the government had to build him a special house outside of town limits because when he snored in his old house, which was in the town center, the foundations of nearby houses shook and his neighbors couldn't sleep. Ibe said Kill-We toured all the schools in the North showing off his prowess—splitting logs of wood with his bare hands and breaking cement blocks with the edge of his palm.

Ibe said that down the street from the house where they lived in the North also lived two *men* who were not really men but women. They walked like women, they tied wrappers on their chests, they waved their hands about like women when they talked and their eyes were ringed with kohl and they painted their fingernails and toenails bright red with nail polish. According to Ibe, at night important and rich men in gleaming black Mercedes-Benz cars came to visit the men who were not really men but women and take them out to town. The men who were not really men but women would return in the early hours of the morning heavily loaded with gifts. They would go to the market and buy stuff to cook. They made such delicious chicken stew with lots of thyme, curry, *tomapep*, and pure groundnut oil; one could smell the aroma of their stew a mile away.

Ibe said that entertainers brought monkeys, hyenas, and baboons to perform in the market. Some of the monkeys were dressed up in ties and some dressed up as women. The monkeys performed dancing tricks. At the command of their owner they would lie down and jerk their waists around like common *karuwa*.

Ibe said it was fine to steal from idols because there was only one God. Idols were blind, they could not see, they were dumb and could not speak. We would wander away from the Family House to where three roads intersected to pick up shiny coins left there by idol worshippers for good luck. He would boldly pick up the pennies, three-penny and five-penny coins. He would kick aside and upturn little sacrificial earthenware pots that contained palm oil and little dead chicks. He would gather all the coins and we would use the money to rent chopper bicycles from the bicycle repairer. We would spend the remainder of the money to buy *suya* beef kebab. He would take a bite and complain, *kai northern suya is best I would not eat this suya for free in the North.*

Ibe said idols had no tongues and it was good to steal from

them though he did believe in magic. He said most drivers that plied the road in the northern part of the country had special magical powers that helped them vanish if they were involved in an accident. At the point at which their vehicle collided with another, their magical power made them vanish and then they would come walking toward the wrecked car from the opposite direction without a scratch. Ibe said he would get this amulet as soon as he was old enough to drive. He said he had tried to drive but was not tall enough to see through the windshield while seated.

Ibe said we were going on a big *mission*. We were going to be like Harrison Ford in *The Temple of Doom*. We both wore pretend helmets that he had made from foolscap sheets. Ibe was the leader of the expedition. We passed the area where three roads intersected. We left the major road. We headed toward the outskirts. Facing us was a small building. It was no bigger than a small shed. It was held up by solid timber pillars on four sides and roofed with corrugated iron sheets now turning rusty. Inside was a large mud sculpture of a matronly figure of a woman carrying newborn babies in both hands. Behind her were bottles of Mirinda, Crush, and Fanta. So many bottles. Some looked like they had been there for a long time; their crown corks were getting rusty. Fresh and cooked eggs lay around. There were lots of shiny coins everywhere; some half hidden in different crevices on the mud sculpture, and there were cowry shells too. On the ground and lying around were different colors and makes of plastic baby dolls and sweets and toffee. Ibe said that these were things left for the goddess by ignorant women who wanted babies. Ibe said that men and women made babies by sleeping together. Ibe said *let the mission begin*. Ibe put a couple of sweets in his mouth and told me to do the same. I put a Hacks in my mouth but spat it out when he wasn't looking. I did not like its peppery taste. Ibe began to scoop coins into his pockets. What are you waiting for? he asked. This is free money. I took a few coins and then we heard approaching footsteps and we fled.

Ibe said we should go to the cinema and watch an Indian movie starring Amitabh Bachchan or Dharmendra. Ibe said Indian actresses were the most beautiful women in the whole wide world. He said they were even more beautiful when they were dancing and that sometimes in the movies while they were dancing, it would start to rain and what luck this was because the rain would plaster their wet saris to their skin and one could catch a glimpse of their breasts.

Ibe paid for the movie with the money we got from the *mission*. Ibe bought *suya*, Ibe bought Fanta, Ibe bought Wall's ice cream, Ibe bought FanYogo, Ibe bought Fan ice orange slush, Ibe bought *guguru*, Ibe bought *epa*. Ibe said we should walk into the movie theater like Harrison Ford walking into the Temple of Doom, we should walk in with a swagger and we should be swaying from side to side because no one could stop us. We did.

Ibe's stomach is distended and swollen like that of Baba-Uwa the *otapiapia* seller who wears a false beard and pads up his stomach with old clothes and dances around the neighborhood of the Family House screaming *only one drop, only one drop* is all you need to kill the cockroach, the mosquito, the lice, the mice, the ant, and the bedbug bugging your life, only one drop of *otapiapia* is all you need.

Ibe said I should come close. I go closer to him. Ibe is sweating. Ibe is clutching his stomach like some pregnant woman holding her jiggling stomach as she rushes to catch a *danfo* bus. Ibe says we must keep our secrets secret. Ibe said the difference between men and women is that men can keep secrets. Ibe's breath is stinky, smelly and damp and green and fetid like the shrine of the goddess. Ibe said do not breathe a word of what happened to anybody. Ibe's breathing is coming out with some difficulty like that of an old transport lorry.

Ibe said put your right hand on the left part of your chest and swear that you'll keep our secret secret. I do as Ibe says.

I say to myself, *What if I do not reveal the secret and Ibe dies?*

Ibe's mom said the Aladura prophetess who wears a white soutane and walks by the family house every early morning chanting *Jehovah El morija yaba sha sha sha* and clanging away on her little silver bell told her Ibe was going to live but she needed to buy a white cow and go with her to the Atlantic Ocean to drown the cow in the center of the ocean. This way the cow's soul would be taken in exchange for Ibe's.

Ibe's mom said she knew who was responsible for Ibe's sickness. She said it was not an *ordinary* sickness. She said it was the evil *karuwa* that her husband had brought into their marriage bed to stain her marriage bed that wanted to kill her first and only son so that she would leave her marriage empty-handed.

She said when Ibe was born a prophet had told her that Ibe's star was so bright its brightness was blinding. She said star destroyers had seen how great her son was going to be and were planning to kill him to stop his star from shining.

Ibe's mom said she was going to consult Nurse Eliza. Nobody knew if Nurse Eliza ever attended a nursing school. People said when she was growing up someone had told her that she looked and walked like a nurse and she had taken those words to heart and had started out without any training by prescribing Panadol for every illness. Now she had graduated to administering injections.

Nurse Eliza said that Ibe's blood was poisoned. She said Ibe's blood required *flushing*. She said Ibe would need to drain all the blood in his body because it was contaminated and it needed to be flushed out and replaced with fresh blood. She said she would need to buy blood from healthy donors, not the hepatitis-contaminated blood sold by junkies and prostitutes who hung around the General Hospital. She asked for a large amount of money. She said blood was expensive because *blood is life*.

I am a married widow, Ibe's mother said. I have no money.

In that case I will just place the boy on a drip, Nurse Eliza said, and hooked Ibe up on a drip. The rusty metal pole of the drip set one's teeth on edge as it was dragged across the concrete floor of the Family House.

Grandfather said Ibe's mom was a stupid woman. He said she was playing with her son's life. He said it was her stupidity that had made her run away from her husband's house because her husband had a concubine. He said if Ibe died because of her carelessness then she had truly left the marriage empty-handed.

Grandfather said if Ibe's mom knew what was good for her, she should carry Ibe and start running to Faith Hospital.

Ibe's mom said that nobody goes to Faith Hospital anymore, that the owner belonged to a blood-sucking secret cult and that people went into his hospital alive and came back dead.

Grandfather said in that case call my friend Doctor Williams.

Doctor Williams said he was no longer practicing. He said his hands shook but that he would come and take a look at the boy.

Doctor Williams said Ibe had appendicitis and that it was liable to burst any moment from now if the boy was not rushed to the hospital to get that thing cut off. Doctor Williams said cutting off an appendix was as easy as cutting off the neck of a chicken, any doctor could do it.

Ibe said he was proud of the little pink scar under his belly. Ibe said appendicitis was caused by swallowing orange and guava seeds instead of spitting them out. If one didn't spit them out they accumulated and after some time one's appendix began to swell.

Ibe said he had told the doctor that he wanted to watch while they cut his stomach open to remove the appendix. Ibe said he told the doctor he was not afraid of pain and had refused to be sedated. He said first he had pretended to close his eyes, then he had opened both eyes and had watched the doctor open up his stomach and cut out the appendix with a surgical blade and tie up the loose ends. Ibe said the doctor had placed multicolored threads inside the different parts of his intestine as he cut. He said he had asked the doctor why he did this and the doctor had said so that I will not be confused by your internal organs and cut your big intestine instead of your appendix.

Ibe said that while he was lying in bed sick he had gone to heaven and had seen God face-to-face. Ibe said God had a long white beard that reached down to God's feet and swept the ground as God floated around in cream-colored bell-bottom pants.

Ibe said he now had the secret of death in his pocket. Ibe said he was never going to die because he had died once and that was the way it was because it was written that *you can only die once and after that eternal life.*

Ibe said before he died he saw people carrying his corpse inside a small coffin. Ibe said he was both inside the coffin and yet outside of the coffin. He said he could still remember snatches from the song the people carrying his corpse were singing:

Ona, ona, nudo, nudo
Onabagonu ebe osi bia
Onwu, onwu, onwu.

Ibe said God was really angry when he was brought to the throne of judgment. Ibe said God asked the people who had brought him why they had brought before his throne this young boy who still had a lot of work to do on God's good earth and was destined to live until the evening of his days. God told them to send Ibe back to the world because it wasn't yet Ibe's time to die. Ibe said when he opened his eyes he was in the hospital wearing a white gown.

Ibe said that everything in heaven was white with the exception of God's cream-colored trousers. The cloud through which God walked was white. God's long beard, which touched God's feet, was white, the angels were all white in color and the trumpets through which they blew the hymn *Hosanna in the Highest* also gleamed white.

I said to Ibe, I know what caused your sickness, what made your belly swell. It was the sweets and money we took from the shrine of the goddess when we went on the *mission*.

Ibe told me to shut my mouth. Ibe said God had sent him back from the dead because he was not afraid of idols. He believed in only one God. Do you think God would have allowed me to come back from the dead if God didn't like the work I was doing here on earth?

Ibe's mom had a new spring in her footsteps. She said the *foolish man* has written, referring to Ibe's dad. The foolish man is now begging. The foolish man has carried both oil and water and now knows which is heavier.

Grandfather said she should shut up and stop making a fool of herself and start packing her things so she could return quietly to her husband's house.

GRAMOPHONE

Whenever the uncle we all called Gramophone, behind his back, walked into any room with a radio on or some music playing, it was immediately turned down or turned off. He would sometimes use two fingers to block both ears when loud music from the record store down the road wafted into the Family House. He was called Gramophone because he would clean and dust every part of the sitting room but would not go near or touch Grandfather's four-in-one Sanyo stereo. When this was pointed out to him once, he shrank back and said he could dust and clean everything in the sitting room but not *that Gramophone*, he said, pointing to the Sanyo stereo. We were warned not to whistle songs around him. Whistling was not encouraged in the Family House at any rate, whistling in the daytime was said to attract snakes while whistling at night attracted evil spirits.

He sought refuge in the Family House many years ago, having killed a man or, as we were told, he had not actually killed the man but the man had died from their encounter and he had had to flee from the village at night. He knew that there was only one place on this earth where no arm no matter how long could reach him, and that was the Family House.

Anytime someone sang any popular song around him, he would cover both ears with his hands like a little child that did not want to hear or listen to an instruction. On days that Grandpa was happy, he hung the loudspeaker of his Sanyo stereo on the outside wall of the house facing the street so that passersby could hear the music playing. Many would stand and listen to the music for a while. Grandpa usually did this when a new LP was released by any of the popular musicians. When a new LP was released, Grandpa bought the record and played it over and over again while a small crowd stood outside enjoying the music. Some in the crowd whispered that this was what it meant to be a rich man. They praised Grandpa for not being selfish. He actually spreads his wealth, so that even those who have no music system can stand in front of his house and enjoy the music, they said.

On such days Gramophone would go to his room and plug his ears with cotton wool and would not emerge until late at night, when the hubbub had died down and the music turned off. When he emerged his eyes would be red and would appear as if he had just finished crying. Those who knew in the Family House would shake their heads. They were the ones who told us his story in bits and pieces, but at the heart of the story was a gramophone record player.

He used to live in the village and was the first man to buy a gramophone record player. His nickname back then was Cash. He was also the owner of I Sold in Cash Provision Store.

In the evenings when people were back from the farms and had finished the day's business, they would sit outside their homes to take in the cool night breeze. Cash would tie his gramophone to the passenger seat of his bicycle and would pedal slowly through the village. As he pedaled past homes, people would call out Cash, Cash. If it was their lucky day, he would gently alight from his bicycle, untie his gramophone. A table would be produced and a piece of antimacassar spread on top of the table on which he would then gently place the gramophone like the special guest that it was. His hosts for the evening would request whatever record they wanted played. A favorite was a play featuring Mama Jigida and Papa Jigida, a bickering couple who quarreled all the time because Papa Jigida was always broke. Sometimes people requested some local musical star. Cash would search through his collection and say, *I don't have the record by that particular musician but I have this one and they both play their guitar in the same way. Listen to it, you'll like it.*

Cash was always a welcome guest and people would bring out their best drinks and kola nuts to entertain him. A few would even put some money by the record changer for him to buy batteries. For many, just having the gramophone sitting there was enough. For first-timers Cash would flip through his pack of LPs arranged in a carton and pick out something. He would bring out the LP, dust it with an orange cotton handkerchief, and gingerly place the record in the changer. First there was a little crackle as the pin scratched the record and then the voices would begin to sing or talk and would float into the surrounding inky darkness.

Whoever thought of putting people in that box must indeed be a wizard, one of the householders would remark.

That is what I keep telling our people, the white people have their own witchcraft but they don't kill their brothers and sisters with it, they invent things like the airplane and the car and this gramophone.

At this point a bottle of half-drunk aromatic schnapps still in its original carton would appear, and drinking would commence while the gramophone made music. Cash would occasionally bring out a record to play. He would begin by introducing the musician. Some of the artists were from the Congo and sang in Lingala. Even though Cash had never been to the Congo he would sometimes translate these songs, especially after a few shots of schnapps:

> I am but a poor orphan
> My mother saved and scraped to buy me a guitar
> I will never forget my mother's sacrifice
> I will play this guitar until I die.

Rotate Provision and Fancy Store was everything Cash Provision Store wasn't. Take the word *Fancy* that was a part of its name. People wondered what the word *Fancy* meant at first, but were not left to wonder for long. Not only did Rotate stock and sell provisions, but he also sold baby clothes, and women's hats and gowns and shoes—these were the fancy goods, according to him.

Cash prided himself on the fact that he sold in cash, hence his nickname, as opposed to credit. Rotate did not mind offering credit and would quickly write down the customer's name and how much was owed in a blue-ruled Olympic Exercise notebook. The only proviso was that customers had to pay a little against what they owed before he could offer more credit.

Rotate installed his own gramophone in his store and hung both loudspeakers from the door. His gramophone was always playing music. He played not only highlife, but also some Western music by KC and the Sunshine Band and Sonya Spence and Don Williams and Skeeter Davis and Bobby Bare.

A bottle of watered-down gin filled with anti-malaria herbs was placed on a table in the store. Customers who had no money could have a free shot of watered-down gin, listen to music, and chat. Some ended up buying an item even if it was just a cigarette.

While Cash closed his store as soon as darkness came, Rotate lived in his store and encouraged people to knock on his window at any time if they needed to buy something. Rotate also had a medicine box out of which he sold tablets. *Just tell him what ails you and he'll mix some tablets that'll cure you*, people said about Rotate.

People no longer talked in whispers about how Rotate got his name or made the money with which he opened his Provision and Fancy Store. They all knew he had made his money from a marijuana farm. When news of the farm reached the ears of the police, a detachment of policemen was sent to arrest him. According to people who were there, the police inspector who led the team had asked Rotate if he did not know that it was illegal to plant marijuana.

"No, sir, I did nothing wrong. I was only practicing crop rotation."

"What do you mean by crop rotation?"

"Well, sir, in school we were taught in agricultural science that it was not good for the soil to plant only one kind of crop from year to year so I decided to rotate the crops. Yam last year, marijuana this year, and corn next year," he shot back.

He was arrested and detained at the police headquarters, but he bribed the police and was released.

When Gramophone heard that another store had opened he went to congratulate the new owner and even sat down ready to share drinks. He knew Rotate's story. Unlike Rotate, he had made his own money by using his bicycle to ferry items to distant markets for female traders. But he believed in live and let live. Rotate did not offer Cash any drinks. According to Cash, the man had rejected his extended hand of fellowship.

Cash began to worry when he noticed that items on his shelf were beginning to expire without being sold. Biscuits, tea bags, tins of milk all sat on the shelves until they expired. He stopped moving around with his gramophone in the evenings to people's homes, preferring to stay in his store instead and play the records in the hope that customers would come in to buy. Rotate's store on the other hand was attracting the younger crowd, who had money to spend and spent it quickly, unlike the older people who counted every penny and loved to haggle.

Cash began to introduce new things. He now sold *chin-chin* and *puff-puff* and buns in a glass-sided display box glass, but Rotate had *beer-beef*—chunky pieces of beef spiced up and fried until they were really dry and filled the mouth—when chewed they were said to enhance the taste of beer on the tongue. Rotate sold sausage rolls, which had the advantage of never going bad. Rotate only bought and sold certain items during certain seasons. Schoolbooks and exercise books when school resumed in September, machetes and hoes at the start of the farming season, raincoats and boots at the start of the rainy season, and Robb, Mentholatum, and Vicks inhaler when the harmattan season set in. Whereas Cash used to pile up all the items in his store even when they were out of season and sometimes even sold brown and faded exercise books to pupils at the beginning of the school year, the stuff from Rotate's store always smelled fresh and new.

And then Rotate bought a Yamaha motorcycle, an Electric 125. It was electric blue in color and flew through the dusty village footpaths like a bird. It made Cash's Whitehorse Raleigh bicycle look shabby and prehistoric.

People began to talk about the fall of Cash and the rise of Rotate. Cash had a framed picture in his store that showed two men. In one half of the picture, the man who sold in cash was smiling and looking prosperous in a green jacket and a fine waistcoat with a gold watch dangling from a chain and gold coins all around him. The other man who sold on credit was dressed in rags and looked haggard. All around him were the signs of his poverty; a rat nibbled at a piece of dry cheese in a corner of the store. A wag suggested that Cash should change his name to Mr. Credit.

Someone came and whispered to Cash that the reason his former customers were running away from his store was that Rotate had been spreading terrible rumors about him. He said that Rotate told people that he opened the soft drinks he sold and mixed them with water in order to get more drinks, that he duplicated keys to padlocks before he sold them.

Cash was angry when he heard these stories and decided to confront Rotate. His plan was to tell Rotate that the sky was wide enough for every manner and specie of bird to fly without running into each other or knocking each other down with their wings. His plan was to tell Rotate that they could indeed practice *rotation* in their business by taking turns to sell certain items so that they didn't create a glut. But Cash's visit was unsuccessful. Rotate rebuffed him, telling Cash— *There is no paddy in the jungle, you mind your business, I mind my own. Every man for himself, God for us all.*

One day there was an early-morning police raid on Rotate. They knew exactly where to look and they found wraps of marijuana in empty giant tins of cocoa beverage. According to some people, the leader of the team had told Rotate to give out everything in his store because this time he was not coming back.

But Rotate did come back after three weeks and he promptly declared total war on Cash, claiming that Cash had ratted him out. Rotate returned from detention red-eyed. He said he was going to wipe out his enemies once and for all. *When you kill a snake, there is no need to leave the head lying around, you must sever the head and bury it in a deep pit*, he boasted. He told his customers to buy only from him; even if there was something they needed and he didn't have it, he would buy it for them the next time he went to the market.

According to Rotate, there were only two kinds of people in this world, those who were for Rotate and those who were against him. He said that there was no way the police would have known where he kept his marijuana cache if someone had not worked as an *informant*. He said if his enemies were jealous because he was the owner of an ordinary motorcycle, then what were they going to do when he bought the fully air-conditioned Peugeot 504 station wagon that he was going to buy soon. Though Rotate had dropped out of school early in form three in secondary school, he still threw around terms from the various subjects he had studied in school and justified his nefarious trade in marijuana by quoting the law of demand and supply. He said having only one store in the village was the equivalent of creating a monopoly. He said he believed in democracy, which was why he played his gramophone for all, unlike Cash, who only played for his favorites. He said he was planning on expanding his business and bringing democracy to the village. He planned to expand his business and open a full-fledged boutique selling ladies' and children's clothes and would also open a chemist shop that would sell medications. He said he was practicing what he had learned in his business methods class in school.

Cash did his best to reach out to Rotate. He sent a couple of individuals who were close to Rotate, the people who bought marijuana from him. Rotate said to them, "The police told me that the person who told them about me and my business told them to lock me up for good, that he did not want them to ever release me from detention. Think of what would have happened if I was never released. Who else could possibly tell them that?"

Soon after his release, Rotate bought an electric generator and a fridge and began to sell cold drinks. Cash had a gas lamp in his store and this was considered a major boost in a village where darkness descended without warning and was impenetrable and dense. But people also told Rotate that the two records Cash played over and over again were songs in which the musicians talked about enemies. One of the songs had the refrain:

> My enemy, you are not my creator
> You are not the owner of my destiny
> Your hatred of me, and your anger against me will kill you.

We had never seen Grandpa dance, but he always told us that the day when Gramophone got married he would dance and dance. When we asked Grandpa why he did not dance he would respond, *If you give me a reason to dance I will dance. Win a scholarship to study in England and I will dance. If you people give me a good reason to dance I will dance.* The only person that dances for no reason is the madman down the street, and even the madman has a reason, it is only that we don't know his reason. But the day your uncle gets married, I will dance for the whole world to see.

Cash would later tell people that when he walked into Rotate's store that evening, he had gone in to make peace. To talk to Rotate as one man to another. He had hoped that they could work things out and settle their differences once and for all over drinks. When Cash walked into Rotate's shop and greeted Rotate, Rotate did not respond to the greeting but said to Cash:

"You are not yet satisfied with informing on me and setting the police after me. You are not satisfied with spreading rumors about me. You are not satisfied with lowering your prices so that people will stop buying from me and buy from you, no you are not satisfied and now you have come to greet me with juju, or you think I don't know who your juju man is, you think the moment you open your mouth to greet me and I respond I will now become a zombie, and slavishly do all your bidding,"

As Rotate said this he came out of his shop and gave Cash a shove. Cash shoved Rotate back. Rotate slumped and fell to the ground. As he lay on the ground, his entire frame shook a couple of times, a little foamlike thing came out of the side of his mouth, his eyes rolled back into his head, and he stopped breathing.

That night a neighbor came to Cash's house and asked Cash whether he was waiting for the police to come and get him and send him to jail for the rest of his life.

—If you know what is good for you, you better start running to the house they call the Family House. You know the big man's house in the city. No one can touch you there—

That was how Cash came to live in the Family House. He was the one who knew where everything was. If an item was misplaced he knew where to find it. If a lightbulb needed to be fixed or the television antennae needed to be turned or there was a hard task that no one else could do in the Family House, he was the man for the job. He had a bunch of keys with him at all times.

The case did not go away. Rotate's people did not give up. They called the police and Cash was charged in absentia with murder. Grandpa tried persuading them to reduce the charge to manslaughter so Cash could serve a few years in prison and be released, but the family refused. After many years, Rotate's uncle, who was at the head of the family's pursuit of justice, died. His relations who were left were tired of the case and the cost of going to court. Many big stores were now in the village and the story of Cash and Rotate's rivalry seemed like an ancient folktale. Some people from Rotate's family soon sent an emissary to Grandpa that they wanted a settlement. Rotate had died single. The family wanted money to be paid, enough money to cover the cost of him marrying a wife and they wanted many white animals, a white cow, a white goat, a white sheep, a white chicken, or the cash equivalent. Grandpa called them for a meeting and it was negotiated down. Eventually they accepted. They were paid. They in turn paid off the police and told the police to close the case.

We were spending the holidays in the Family House the day the man formerly known as Cash, now Gramophone, got married. Grandpa had given him one of the girls who lived in the house. Her father had owed Grandpa some money and she had come to live in the Family House until the debt was owed. We were told that by the time her father was ready to repay the debt the girl said she did not want to return to her father's house anymore or some other person said that her father had died and nobody bothered to come for the girl after that.

On the day that Gramophone got married, there was a big party in the Family House. The entire street was invited and there was lots of music, but he did not block his ears when he was led out to dance with the bride. Grandpa also danced and danced. The kids from the poorer houses were so excited to have bottles of soft drinks to themselves. They were urged to drink as many as they wanted. Some of them had so many drinks and poured some away and screamed to each other excitedly about pouring a half-finished bottle of soft drink away.

I remember that at some point in the night the man in charge of the music had wanted to turn off the music, but Grandpa had instructed that the music be played until morning. As we rolled in our sleep toward morning we could still hear the music playing in front of the family house.

In time Gramophone/Cash had children and told Grandpa that he wanted to return to the village. This is your home now, Grandpa said to him. His children soon joined the many children who lived in the Family House and would grow up to work for Grandpa.

UNCLE AYA

They came from every part of the city. Some came all the way from the surrounding villages and towns. Others had walked long distances and their sweaty feet had accumulated a fine coating of dust. A few had brought cooking utensils and some foodstuffs along with kerosene stoves. The poorer ones had brought along firewood and sawdust to light a fire and cook with.

Grandfather always said that in a great man's house you'll find at least one eccentric person. This was his usual response to the antics of Uncle Aya. Grandpa was of the view that each great household had both good and bad people. You'll find wise men, lawyers, doctors, and the occasional mad fellow or eccentric. He said Uncle Aya was the eccentric in our great household and urged members of the household to at least accommodate his eccentricities.

A few years back Uncle Aya had started corresponding with a certain Pastor Jonah from the West Indies who was also founder of End of the World Ministries. Uncle Aya would sometimes enlist us to help distribute their badly printed tracts, the black ink spilling from the words and the words aslant, some of the printed words smudged beyond recognition—inviting people to their crusades, healing crusades, everyday crusades, miracle crusades, Bible crusades. They usually used a large open space almost the size of a football field behind the Family House. This was where they showed *Photo-Drama of the First Day of Creation*. Not really a movie as such but moving photo slides. It showed how the earth was created from darkness. I recall some of the conversation around us as the images flashed.

—So someone was there with a film camera filming God as he made the earth?—

—Wonders will never end. So filmmaking was invented before man was created?—

—Or was God holding a camera as he was creating the earth?—

End of the World Ministries had many teachings that made it soon begin to attract a lot of members. They believed that it was justified to drink alcohol but not justified to get drunk because Paul had written to Timothy to drink a little wine for the sake of his stomach. They said that somewhere in the Bible God had said, *Wine makes the heart of mortal man to rejoice.*

They believed it was not a sin to have more than one wife if you had married both wives before coming into *knowledge*. That was the expression they used when talking about their past lives before they became members.

—I used to be a violent criminal before I came into *knowledge*, but I am now a changed person since I came into the knowledge—a new member would say during Testimony Time.

They said all members shared everything and one should be happy to give the shirt off one's back to another member of the church. They did not believe in elaborate funerals—a simple coffin, a few songs about waking up to behold the glory of the Father in heaven, and the burial. This was so loved by the poor because funeral expenses were usually high and those who could not bury their dead relations elaborately always faced one misfortune or another. But their greatest belief, the one that attracted more and more people to the group, was their belief that the world was coming to an end on a certain date.

They kept Sundays holy. There was to be no cooking, no lighted fire for cooking purposes, no raised voices, no eating or drinking till after the service, no work only rest, prayer, reading of the word, and groaning in the spirit and prophesying. If unfortunately a member died it was not to be announced on a Sunday. In fact it was kept a secret and no member's family ever said that a member had died on a Sunday. Nothing must taint the holiness of Sunday.

I remember that for their first miracle crusade, which was to be led by Pastor Jonah, Uncle Aya had printed a lot of flyers and they had gone through the town with raised banners calling on members of the public to come with all their illnesses to the crusade ground and be healed by the man who had raised the dead in his home country, this was Pastor Jonah.

They had been attacked when they went to the Beggars Lane, the place where the beggars lined up to receive alms, to invite the blind and lame beggars to come to the healing crusade in order to be healed. The king of the beggars had told the beggars to attack Uncle Aya's group with sticks and stones.

—Did we tell you we want to be healed? Why do you want to deprive us of our means of livelihood?—

The members of the End of the World Ministries had returned from the event very excited. According to them, this was *persecution*, they had been persecuted for their beliefs and this was the final sign that would occur before the end of the world.

But that particular crusade was never held because Pastor Jonah took ill. He had caught malaria and lay on a narrow iron bed in Uncle Aya's room sweating heavily and muttering in a strange language. His thick giant-typeface Bible (the Amplified Version with Annotations and Comprehensive Concordance) lay closed beside him, lying side by side with the immobile slides of *Photo-Drama of the First Day of Creation*. When he burst out in a foreign tongue, Uncle Aya would come closer to him, holding an open exercise book and a pen poised to jot down his words which he declared were words of prophecy.

"Don't let this your pastor die in my house, you better take him to the hospital," Grandfather told Uncle Aya.

"How can he die? Have you not heard that he raised the dead in his home country?"

"Well, if he dies here there'll be no one to raise him from the dead. Besides, why can't he help himself by healing himself of the malaria that is about to kill him."

"He is not suffering from malaria; he is in a trance receiving prophetic messages from God."

Eventually, Pastor Jonah recovered from the malaria attack and went back to the West Indies. Then he returned again, and they were preparing for the greatest event of all—the ending of the world. They said the world was going to end on a certain date at night. Probably on the first of September. They had already given out the date and they began encouraging their members to give out all of their material things, in fact all their earthly property, because they were all going up to heaven, and in heaven they would not need earthly things anymore. They were encouraged to sell what they could and bring the proceeds to Pastor Jonah. They were told to donate the things that they couldn't immediately sell. Gold and silver were always welcome as donations to the church.

The fame of the ministry soon spread and many people began to attend their prayer meetings.

—I was unemployed but now I don't have to worry about getting a job anymore because the world will end on the first of September. When I get to heaven I never have to work again because all we will do from morning to night and night to morning is sing Hosanna in the highest with Angel Michael and the rest of the heavenly hosts—

—I was always worrying about having a baby for my husband but I am not worried anymore because the world is coming to an end, I don't want a pregnancy to stand between me and heaven—

—I have sold my uncompleted building and given the money to the church, according to Pastor Jonah, there are many mansions in heaven and we will pick and choose the one we want—

—I just got a loan but I have given the money to the church because I am leaving for heaven and I will not need to repay the loan—

And so many were already disposing of anything that would stand as an encumbrance to heaven. I remember that Grandfather's response to all of this had been to quote from the prayer book of the Anglican Church, the part that said— *World without End Amen*. Grandfather had also remarked that if the heaven was going to fall and cover the earth it shouldn't be of concern to only one individual but should be the concern of all who lived here on earth under the sky.

When Pastor Jonah and Uncle Aya were asked how the world was going to end, was it by water like the flood of Noah or was it by fire because the Bible refers to God as a consuming fire, they both replied that they did not know. The only thing they said they knew was that God was going to take his people, the members of the church who had come to knowledge, up into heaven before unleashing his judgment on those who were left on earth.

Uncle Aya, we were told, had been a weird one since he was little. It was said that when he was younger and chickens were being killed to make stew for Christmas celebrations, he would gather the other children in the house around the slaughtered chicken and tell the kids to close their eyes while he prayed for the dead chickens. He told the other children that chickens had souls and that if he didn't pray for the chickens the chickens would lose both their bodies and their souls. He prayed for sick animals. He would lay hands on them and whisper things. He dreamed dreams and saw visions. While in elementary school, he predicted the death of a classmate from measles.

Grandpa sent him to a boarding school. One day on a school picnic beside a lake, one of his classmates had pushed him into the lake. It took a while before the teacher's attention was called and a senior student dived into the lake and rescued Uncle Aya. The story was that when they brought him out of the lake his stomach was swollen to three times its size. They had to give him mouth-to-mouth resuscitation and then someone suggested pressing his stomach. Water came out of his mouth. He sneezed and came to. When Grandpa heard about the incident, he went and brought him back from the school. They say Grandpa said it was a taboo for him to be the one who buried his children instead of the other way round. After the incident, Uncle Aya began telling stories of the things he had seen while he was underwater. A beautiful place with double-story buildings all constructed with solid gold. He said the buildings sparkled and glittered.

"What happened to the boy is bigger than what his mind can contain, it sure shook up his mind," Grandpa said.

First he was taken to the hospital to see a doctor but the doctor said there was nothing wrong with him, then he was taken to see a prophetess of a white garment church. He began living in the church and wore only flowing white soutanes. He began to see religion in mundane everyday activities. When smoke rose out of the Family House chimney he watched it to see if it went up in a straight line or dispersed. If it went up in a straight line he would say it is acceptable unto the lord, if it curved or dispersed he would say that there was something unholy being cooked. He would go days saying he was on a white fast and would eat only food that was white in color—white corn pap, white bread, white yams, egg whites, and avoid things cooked with oil.

At other times he would insist that before any chicken was slaughtered or any goat or sheep for that matter that he had to pray for its soul and make the sign of the cross across its heart. He would conduct funerals for dead birds and dead lizards and insist that they had souls and he wanted their souls to make heaven.

The story of how much he loved God was usually illustrated with an incident from his childhood. He had been given two coins. The coin with a higher denomination was for him to put in the offering box in church while the smaller coin was for him to buy a Popsicle for himself when he finished at church. As he jumped across an open drain on his way to church, the larger coin flew out of his pocket into the open drain.

Sorry, there goes my Popsicle money, God, he said, and looked up to heaven, your own money is still intact.

Another kid would have said, Sorry, God, but that was your money that just fell into the drain.

The End of the World Ministries wasn't Uncle Aya's first religious movement. Years back he had founded another religious movement that combined the teachings of Islam, Christianity, and Ancestor worship. The movement picked a few of the things that it liked in the different religions and its members were free to pray in any way they saw fit according to the ways of the three religions. They were free to marry more than one wife if they promised to love all the wives equally. They celebrated on Christmas day, fasted during the month of Ramadan, and worshiped ancestors on designated months.

Uncle Aya consulted oracles using divination beads made from the seeds of the African star apple. But he could also see the future when he wore a white soutane and fell into a trance and would claim to see angels who whispered the secrets of men and women into his ears. It was with the syncretic movement that he had first gotten into trouble and nearly got the Family House burned down. He claimed he could see the future. His fame had reached some young military boys who were planning a coup to overthrow the ruling military government. They had come in the dead of night to ask him if their coup was going to be successful. There had been a few attempts in the past to overthrow the military head of state, but he was said to have more than nine lives. Uncle Aya had told them to leave and come back in three days' time and allow him time to fast, do some ablution, and consult the ancestors. When they left, he had dressed up and gone to the director of Military Intelligence to tell him that some young soldiers were planning to overthrow the head of state. The young soldiers were apprehended, because merely thinking of a coup was a punishable offense. They were tried before a military tribunal and sentenced to long jail terms. Some of their fellow soldiers had heard of the ignoble role Uncle Aya had played in the whole affair and had attempted to burn the house down one night. They were in mufti but of course they were soldiers and knew how to move about at night without being heard. The fire was put out before much damage could be done to the house. The attempt had failed and Uncle Aya had to lie really low for a while. And then one day he had bought a little pamphlet by Pastor Jonah from a pavement vendor of used books. He said it was something about the title and the man with a raised fist on the cover that had caught his attention.

The night began with a lot of the members eating the meals they had cooked. There were to be no leftovers, since that would be such a waste because there would be no one to eat the food the next day. People invited others to come over and share their food. And then the eating was soon over and members were instructed to go and change into fresh clothes and to look neat and tidy.

"You dress up when going before a judge. Shouldn't you

dress even better as you go to meet your God?" This was Pastor Jonah encouraging people to go and put on their best clothes.

Soon Uncle Aya appeared wearing well-ironed black pants and a clean white shirt rolled up to his elbows. He ran and swerved through the crowd as he pointed in different directions. "Our savior e dey here?"

"Yes, e dey," the people screamed back while they too pointed in different directions. "Our savior e dey here?" "Yes, e dey." Is our savior here, yes he is here.

There had been yet another incident in Uncle Aya's past when he was nearly killed by soldiers if not for Grandpa's intervention. The government had declared a curfew. By this time Uncle Aya had joined another prophetic church and would routinely go to the church to pass the night. He said that 3:00 AM was when the spirit of God usually visited and that it was important to be in a holy place like the church so that the spirit wouldn't turn back because the place it was visiting was polluted.

On his way back from church he ran into soldiers who pointed their flashlights in his face and asked:

"Who goes there? What is your name? Why are you out at this time? Did you not hear of the curfew?"

"I am the man of God and I am coming back from the Lord's errand like Angel Gabriel."

"Kneel down there and start crawling on your knees."

"I kneel for no mortal. I only kneel for my maker," Uncle Aya replied.

"Then prepare to meet your maker," one of the soldiers said, and fired his gun.

Uncle Aya raised his hand into the air and screamed, "Oh my Lord and my God, receive the soul of your servant!"

But Uncle Aya was not dead. The soldier had shot into the air and was only having fun. The soldier was in fact drunk.

Uncle Aya had screamed, thinking he had been shot.

Grandfather heard the scream and assumed he had been shot and ran out, for this was happening close to the house.

"Who are you?" one of the soldiers asked.

"I am his father," Grandfather said, pointing at Uncle Aya, who was by now kneeling on the ground.

"You must be God then, because he told us his father is in heaven."

"Who is your commander?" Grandfather asked.

"Why do you want to know?" the drunk soldier said, and rushed at Grandfather and hit him on the head with his Mark 4 rifle.

"You will pay dearly for this," Grandfather said, holding his head, which was already bleeding.

And the soldiers looked at themselves, gathered their stuff, and fled.

This incident happened on the first of September. On September first the next year, Grandfather developed a blinding headache. It was a headache like no other. Black cloths had to be spread on all the windows so no drop of sunlight could penetrate into the house. The headaches were soon to be known as Grandfather's September headaches. They came every September without fail, marking the day he was hit on the head by soldiers with a gun because of Uncle Aya.

Lightning flashed across the sky. They paused in their chorus singing. Many raised their eyes to the sky. It was going to happen, finally.

But it didn't. There was a little drizzle that lasted no longer than three minutes. The type of drizzle known as kerosene rain because of the way it dried up quickly like kerosene.

As light began to erase the darkness and some of the crowd could now see each other clearly, screams began to emanate from the crowd. Uncle Aya announced that Pastor Jonah was going inside the house to seek the face of the Lord and to get answers.

There was a shout of my bicycle here. And over there a shout of my sewing machine. And yonder a shout of my fridge. And even farther down a louder scream of my TV.

—I have given out all my earthly property what am I going to do? How can I continue living? What am I going to tell my neighbors? The world will make me their laughingstock—

Slowly the crowd became angry. First it was sachets of plastic water that were hauled at the house, then someone picked up a piece of stone and hauled it at one of the louvers on the window upstairs. The louver shattered. Others seemed to take a cue and began to haul objects at the house. Uncle Aya fled inside. A voice in the crowd said someone should get petrol so they could burn both the house and the lying pastor down and send the pastor to heaven to go and seek God's face. Another stone scattered yet another windowpane.

And then a shot rang out. Grandfather was standing on the balcony. He was holding his double-barreled gun. He fired off yet another shot into the air, and the crowd fell silent.

"Did your pastor tell you that this was his house? Did he tell you that he built this house or that it belongs to him? Did I join you people in your madness? While you were waiting and praying for the world to end was I not in my bed sleeping? Why should you burn down my house?"

And so the crowd began to disperse. First one person and then another. Until there was nobody left.

ABULE

Even those of us who were considered too young to know knew that Abule's wife was a loose woman who went with other men. It came as no surprise then when one morning her husband took out his double-barreled rifle and began going from house to house threatening to kill all the men who had been sleeping with his wife. She was from a different part of the country. One of the stories told about her people was that it was not uncommon for a husband to entertain a visiting overnight guest with one of his wives. It was considered a gesture of genuine hospitality. If the visitor did a good job the wife would put out a bucket of water in the bathroom for him to take his bath the next morning. If he didn't please the woman, he would have to get his own bathwater for himself the next morning.

The woman's name was Fanti, and she had a little shed where she sold rice and beans and stew and *dodo* and macaroni and pasta. People would stop over on their way to work to buy food and chat. Oftentimes by midafternoon all the food was sold. On days that she didn't sell all she would put the food in a cart and hawk up and down the street. She was jovial and always laughing. She let men touch her. Her husband was a retired daily paid laborer who had worked with the railways. He was a man who walked gingerly and gently, as if he was afraid to tread too hard on the earth. His house had a piazza and he would usually sit on his hammock and drink tea. He was retired and was a pensioner. He responded to the greetings of both old and young with just one phrase—*'Allo dear.*

It was not long before Fanti started selling beer in her shed. She would sell food in the morning and start beer sales in the afternoon. Soon her place became a gathering point for some of the young men who lived on the street. They said she had relationships with at least three or four of the men. What was said of her was that she was the type that could never be satisfied with one man.

It was a gray morning when the first shot rang out. Fanti's husband, Abule, had fired that warning shot in the air. He had his shiny double-barreled gun and was walking down the street with the gun slung over his shoulders. Later people who were close to him would say they heard him muttering the words, *Today is today, it will all end today.*

He stood in front of the house of one of his wife's supposed lovers and screamed his name.

"Come out if you call yourself a man, today is the day it will end." Abule shouted the words out aloud as he held the gleaming rifle and raised it and pointed it at the house.

Doors slammed shut as people went into hiding, women and children running under their beds to hide.

"Come out or I'll come and get you myself. You call yourself a man. Come out if you are a man," he shouted again.

When there was no response he walked to the door, pushed it open, and began to walk down the corridor. No one knows till today how he knew the exact door of the man who was said to be one of his wife's lovers. He was a bricklayer. Abule kicked the door open. The lover was attempting to push the window open to escape when Abule fired off the first round. The shot got the fleeing man in the shoulder. He screamed and fell over the window into the yard. Abule brought out another bullet from the pocket of his dark brown railway-issue overalls. It was shiny, its silver head encased in a red plastic shell. He was walking round to the back of the house to the window where the man he had shot earlier lay when he changed his mind and began striding down the street to another house down the road. The house belonged to another man who was always in the wife's store. He was an *agbero*, a motor park tout; he got a cut from every fare paid by travelers to the driver. He hung around the motor park calling passengers, helping them board, and collecting a commission. He was the one who had insisted that Fanti start selling beer even though she did not have the required license.

Abule walked into the man's house. The man was still in bed. He prodded him with the nozzle of the double barrel. The *agbero* man was not fully awake; he jumped up and rubbed his eyes. Abule cocked his gun and shot him in the head at close range. The man fell back on the bed. There was blood on the unpainted cement wall. Abule walked out.

Only the sound of gunshots broke the silence of the street. All the people on the street were in hiding. There were no screams. Abule was humming a railway work song as he walked back home. His walk was jaunty and springy. He even had a little smile on his face and he licked his thin lips over and over again.

"Come out, Fanti. I have finished your men. Now it is your turn," he said aloud for people to hear.

He went inside to where he kept his bullets and reloaded. He walked into Fanti's bedroom, but she had fled. He stepped out of the house and stepped into the road. He raised his gun and released a shot into the air.

Grandpa heard the shot and came out of the house and looked into the street from the open balcony.

Abule was still shouting and saying that anybody who considered himself man enough should come out. He said those who were sleeping with his wife who called themselves men should come out and show themselves as brave men. He went to the backyard of his house and came out with a half can of gasoline and a box of matches. He walked to the shed where

Fanti sold rice in the daytime and beer in the evenings. He half covered the mouth of the gasoline gallon with one finger as he began to spray the gasoline on the small wooden shed. When he was done spraying he struck a match and the small shed began to blaze. All the while his gun was hanging on his left shoulder. He watched the shed burn for a bit and walked back to his house in fast strides. He stood in his piazza holding his gun. Once more he shouted that anyone who considered himself a man should come outside. The doors remained locked and the street was silent. The street was still empty. Grandfather walked out of the Family House in small, slow steps. He did not walk like someone in a hurry.

Abule, Abule, Grandfather called the name twice. Abule turned; he raised his gun and positioned it, as if about to take a shot. He looked up and noticed it was Grandfather.

"Man of courage, the fearless lion, great warrior, the big wizard," Abule hailed Grandfather.

"Put down your gun and let's talk. Let's talk like two men. If there is any doubt that you are a man of courage I have never been among the doubters."

"It takes a man of courage to drive a train, that dragon that belches smoke from here to Kaura-Namoday."

Grandfather was only flattering Abule. Abule was not a locomotive train driver. He had joined the railways as a laborer and had retired as a lowly laborer but the inflated praise words brought a smile to Abule's parched face.

"Give me the gun," Grandfather said. "Hand it over."

Abule looked at Grandfather and shook his head from side

to side in refusal. He was suddenly transformed into a child refusing to hand over a favorite toy.

"Give me the gun. When you hand me the gun we can talk man to man. I cannot talk with you if you are holding a gun over my head," Grandfather said.

Abule handed over the gun. Grandfather held the gun sideways in the middle, and as if breaking it, cracked the gun open and the two bullets popped out. He put the bullets in his pocket.

Grandfather called out to someone in the Family House to bring over a kettle of tea. The tea was brought over and Grandfather made a cup for Abule. Abule blew into the cup and took a sip.

"You are the only good man in this neighborhood. Since I built my house here they have always troubled me. I suffered during my time in the railways. Carrying heavy items on my bare head in the sun. Pouring gravel on the tracks. Carrying wood for repair of the tracks. I saved every penny to build this house and to marry. I could not marry from my own people because I didn't want trouble, my people and their *wahala*. But they didn't let her rest. Now my life is ruined," Abule said, and began to cry.

"You should not allow a woman to ruin your life," Grandpa said. "You have killed one man. The other man is still alive, he survived. I will talk to the police. They will understand. I will help them understand. Go inside and take a bath and wear fresh clothes. I will contact the police. Don't say a word when they get here, let me handle everything," Grandfather said.

That day we heard a new phrase for the first time. It was our favorite expression for many weeks. Grandpa told the police that Abule had committed *a crime of passion.*

Abule was sent to jail but for only about eighteen months for manslaughter. The *agbero* man was not well liked in the first place. Grandpa put Abule's house up for rent while Abule was in prison, and when Abule came out Grandfather handed over the rent money collected in his absence to him.

"You are the only good man on this street. I have said that before and I say it again," Abule said.

He was thankful but he said he could no longer live on the street. He was old and tired. Being in prison had worsened things. Grandfather offered to buy the house at a ridiculously low price. Abule agreed. He handed the certificate of occupancy to Grandfather. Abule went to live in the village. Grandfather converted the house into shops facing the street and put the shops up for rent.

TATA

By the time Tata lost her third baby at birth, other people in the Family House were calling her a soul stealer. Some people said she was the one stealing the souls of her dead babies. None of the children lived longer than the seventh day. First they stopped drinking breast milk. They began to run a fever, and a few days later they started hiccupping and then died. As the body of the third child was being taken away from the Family House to be buried, people whispered among themselves.

—Poor children, they didn't want to live in this world on the seventh day. Instead of being christened, they are being buried on the day their naming ceremony should have taken place—

—This is no ordinary death. All three children died before they are named—

—The worm eating the apple is inside the apple. I think the woman must be a witch. You know with the soul stealers they don't care once it's your turn you have to bring your own child's soul to be eaten because you have also partaken in the eating of other people's children, that's the law of the coven—

—But what I heard is different. They say you usually have to give them the child whom you love most to show how much loyalty you have to the coven—

—But if she really is a witch, how come she has to sacrifice all three of her children? Is she the only one in the coven?—

—They do it according to rank and seniority. The senior soul stealers don't have to sacrifice their own children. I hear it is also a power thing the more children you sacrifice the more power you have and the earlier you'll attain a higher position—

All the whisperings got to Tata's ears. She was one of the wives in the house. She stopped the men who were carrying the body of the dead baby to the cemetery for burial.

It hadn't been easy for her to conceive either. Most of the female herbalists she went to said she had a hot womb that was too *hot* for a baby to grow in and had given her herbal medications to *cool* the womb.

She carried the dead child to the shrine of the river goddess. She cried to the river goddess. The priestess of the river goddess told her to wait with the body in the shrine. She waited. Later that day the priestess told her to remove her clothes and change into white clothes. She did. She told her to wrap the dead child in a white sheet. She did. She told her to wait by the riverbank. When it was getting to late evening, the river goddess asked her to wade into the water with the dead child. When she got into the middle of the water she saw a figure rising out of the water toward her. She was very fair skinned, a little plump, her face glowed silvery like a fluorescent light, she told Tata to give her the dead baby. Tata handed the baby to her.

—In place of the baby I'll give you something that'll take you places and make you better known than even your husband and all the men. The only thing is that you must promise to venerate my name. Before you start anything you must give honor to my name. And from today you must dress only in white. Everything in your life has to be white. She was requested to drop the dead child into the river. She did. As the child sank, a medium-size mirror floated to the top of the water. Pick up the mirror—she was commanded.

She did.

—This mirror will help you catch soul stealers and wizards. It will help catch thieves. It will help identify any person who commits any crime and denies it. This mirror works better than any detective. All you need to do when people come to you is get a set of drummers to drum and sing my praises, let them sing the praises of the river goddess. As the singing and drumming heighten, bring out the mirror and begin to chant my praises. I will show you who has committed the crime. In fact the perpetrator of the crime will appear in the mirror and all eyes will see them. This mirror will give you wealth. It will make your name known all over the world—

"And will it give me children?" Tata asked.

—No, it will not give you children. Every woman comes to this world with a certain number of children in her womb. You were destined to have three. They are gone—

"What about one, just one child?"

—You will have no children of your own but the noise of children, and people will never depart from your compound—

That was how Tata Mirror got the name Tata Mirror. She returned to the family house and told Grandpa what she was told. Grandpa knew that this was a great business opportunity. He carved out a consultation room from one of the rooms facing the street downstairs. He donated two of the boys in the house to her as drummers. He made a signboard and put it in front of the house. The signboard said: WHATEVER YOU ARE SEARCHING FOR MY MIRROR WILL FIND IT. WITCHES AND WIZARDS, CHILDREN, LOST ITEMS, ETC.

We would later learn to beat those same drums ourselves.

Those who were there when it happened said the first case that was brought to Tata was the young man who died down the street. He was from a polygamous home. He always took the first position in school. He was both senior prefect and sanitation prefect in his secondary school. When he finished secondary school he wanted to go to the university to study medicine but was offered a place to study pharmacy, but medicine was his first love so he decided to wait for a year and then reapply. He got a job as a cashier with a bank. Because he was a levelheaded boy he still lived with his mother. On his way to the bus stop to take a bus to work in the morning people would marvel at the sparkling white shirt he wore.

—That boy's brain is faster than a calculator, I hear—

—Look at the white shirt dazzling like an angel—

—I hear he is going to the university next year to become a doctor—

—He will make a good doctor he is so kind and caring—

—With the kind of money he is earning from the bank some of his mates would go to rent their own apartments so they can drink, smoke, and bring girlfriends home. But just look at him he still lives at home, helping his mother—

—Other kids should learn from him. Nowadays as soon as they are in form two they stop greeting older people. They start flying the collar of their shirts—

One day at work the young man turned to the cashier sitting next to him and said, "I want to take off my tie. It is getting very hot in here."

"Are you sure you don't have a fever?" the other cashier replied. "The air-conditioning is on."

"I really, really, need to take this tie off."

"Go ahead, if you want to, you can, but if the supervisor sees you without a tie you'll be in trouble."

He removed the tie and dropped it on the floor.

"I am still feeling quite hot," he said after a few minutes.

"I think you should go to the first-aid box and take some paracetamol. Or do you want me to call the supervisor so he can excuse you to go and see a doctor?"

"I am not sick. I just feel hot," he said and took off his shirt.

When his colleague noticed that he had pulled off his shirt he rushed to the outer office to call the supervisor. When he came out of the outer office with the supervisor, the cashier was out of his cubicle. He was stark naked. He was fanning himself with his shirt. "I still feel very hot," he kept muttering. All the bank's customers fled the banking hall.

He turned out to be Tata's first major client. His family was called to the bank. He was bundled to the hospital, but the doctor took one look at him and diagnosed his condition as *home trouble*. He said it was not the kind of illness that should be brought to the hospital. The young man was still complaining of heat even though only a blue bedsheet covered him. Someone must have mentioned Tata, because the young man was soon brought to Tata's room in the Family House. His mother was there, so were his father and his father's second wife. The drummers began to pound their drums. We could only peep through the green mosquito netting into the room. In a small earthenware pot on the fire a mixture of water and white loam was boiling angrily.

Tata was clad in a white woven cloth, on her right hand she held a mirror and on the left a fan decorated with chicken feathers. She began to dance and hop about. First on one leg, then on the other one. She spread out both hands the way a bird would spread out its wings and moved around the room in speedy spurts, as if propelled by a force inside of her that eyes couldn't see. Finally she stopped in front of the two wives. The young man was sitting quietly now. He was rocking back and forth. His eyes were glazed, but he had at least stopped screaming about his body being on fire.

"You know yourself, you know who you are. Say what you did to him," Tata said, glaring angrily at both women. They were both sitting on carved wooden chairs.

"If the river goddess reveals you, you'll die. Reveal yourself now or the repercussion will be dire."

Both women shrank back. Tata began to dance once again as the drums picked up a beat and increased its tempo. The music of the drums was heady, it did something to the spirit, first it was mournful, then it turned stirring and hypnotic, even.

Tata began to peer into her mirror. She looked into the mirror and covered her eyes, as if frightened by what she saw. She looked into the mirror again. She laughed, but there was no joy in her laughter.

Two aluminum cups were dipped into the boiling pot of clay and given to the women to drink from. The younger wife drank first. As she drank she was urged on by Tata. Drink everything. Those who have nothing to hide find this to be a refreshing drink. Those who have something to hide think it poison. Drink and drain the cup. It was now the turn of the boy's mother. She was reluctant to drink.

"Why do I need to drink? I am not on trial. It is my own son they are trying to kill."

"Yes, which is the more reason for you to drink and show the whole world that you have clean hands."

"I have nothing to hide. I bore him. The world knows that I can never harm a child that came out of my own womb. I carried him for nine months."

"Are you afraid to drink?"

"No, I have nothing to be afraid of. I have not done anything."

"Then drink it."

"I don't want to drink on an empty stomach. I have not eaten since I heard of my son's troubles."

"It is like food. Consider this milk from the river goddess."

By this time the drums had become silent. Tata looked into her mirror and shook her head. The boy's mother drank. She was urged to drain the cup. She drank and drained the cup and then she began to talk.

"It was me who did it. I cooked my son. I boiled him. They said I had to do it. They said I had taken part in the killing of other people's children and that it was now my turn. They said I should bring them the son I loved most. I refused; I told them he was my life my future, my retirement hope. They said I would get a big title. They said I would be promoted. They told me I would be cruising around in a pleasure car in our world. I was reluctant to do it but I was persuaded."

"Can he be cured? Can he still return?" the father of the boy asked.

"He has been cooked and eaten. All that while he was screaming about being hot he was being boiled in a cauldron."

The boy's father spoke again, he was pleading.

"You must be able to do something. Beg the goddess for us, we will sacrifice whatever she wants to save my son."

"It is too late," Tata said. "Your son is gone. They have taken his spirit. This is a mere husk you are looking at."

Before his burial a mob gathered and said they wanted to lynch his mother. She was not lynched. One of her brothers, a pastor in a white garment church, would take her away for deliverance from the spirit of witchcraft. This same brother of hers would one day spit at the Family House while walking past it and refer to the house as a demonic and fetish house. Her husband would accuse Tata of putting strange liquids in a cup and forcing his wife to drink it.

Tata's fame as a witch catcher grew. Every day, there was drumming in the house. And soon enough a new group of people began living in the house. These were people who had confessed their witchcraft but were left behind out of shame by their families.

How can they follow us back home after the evil they have done? their families asked. Grandpa had not envisaged this fallout from Tata's new line of business, but he was happy about it. New hands meant more working hands, and more money. These men and women became his washermen. They washed, starched, and ironed neighborhood laundry for a pittance. Initially a few people on the street were reluctant to bring their laundry to the Family House but the price was too good and whites came back sparkling, smelling clean and well ironed. Yet people talked.

—It is even stated in the holy books that a witch should not live but die—

—These are not witches anymore. Once a witch has confessed, all her power is gone—

—How do you know? Have you been a witch before?—

—No, but one knows things. Witchcraft is like a secret society. Once you reveal their secrets, they expel you—

—Yes, they expel you but you still have their secrets with you—

—You can tell that these people who live in that house still have supernatural powers—

—Why do you say that?—

—They wash clothes and do all kinds of domestic work but they never get tired. And look at the clothes they launder for people, always clean and sparkling. They have sent the other washermen out of business—

—They act strange. They don't make eye contact, always staring at the ground. They never speak. They are always working—

—I think they are just grateful to have a place to stay. They are grateful to be alive—

—After all the lives they took and all the evil they have committed in their coven they should just let them die—

—Well, you know how they are in that house. Anything that'll make them money they are for it—

—Money, money, that is all they know—

Tata's business continued to boom. Communities would invite her to come and consult her mirror as to the reason why their sons and daughters were not getting ahead, why were they not growing like other communities. Sometimes she would ask them to cut down a large iroko tree in the center of the town and name the top of the tree the meeting place for soul stealers and wizards. Some would want to know why their market was not big or did not attract people like other markets. She would tell them that soul stealers bought and sold there at night and did not want people to trample on their space in the daytime. Her drummers would beat their drums, she would dance, she would prance around and then she would command one of her boys to start digging somewhere in the market. They would unearth a large pot covered with moss and cowrie shells. She would tell them that this pot was buried by soul stealers. And soon thereafter the market began to boom.

Tata would come back home with gifts of money and drinks. Once she came back with two cows. Grandpa said he didn't know anything about rearing cows and called a passing cattle herder from the cattle-rearing tribe to come and take the cows away. This honest cattle herder would return many years later with over a hundred cows for Grandpa.

Yet tongues wagged. People were angry at Tata's fame and Grandpa's growing wealth.

—She must be a witch herself, otherwise where does she get all her powers from?—

—She might be a witch; it is just that her witchcraft power is bigger than that of the people she was making to confess—

—Nothing lasts forever. Witchcraft has been existing since the beginning of time—

—Even the white man has his own witchcraft, only theirs is white witchcraft and they use it to invent great things like airplanes and ships—

—Our people use theirs to pull other people down, that is the problem—

As Tata's fame grew, so did the whispering and gossip. By this time the mirror looked worn and aged. One day a young woman came to the Family House with the dead body of her young child. The child must have been about two years old. She said she was on her way back from spending some time with her mother-in-law when she was stopped by an older woman whom she didn't know so well. She was carrying her baby on her back. The older woman told her to wait, that she needed to adjust the neck of her sleeping baby. The older woman helped her adjust the baby's neck and then touched the baby on the neck and remarked that the baby was one chubby child. She thanked the old woman and began to walk home. A few minutes later, the baby began to cry, he was sweating profusely. By the time she got home the baby was crying even harder and was gasping for breath. She gave the baby a cold bath and without toweling him dry brought him into her room and laid him under the fan. She stepped out of the room to get a little something to eat. When she stepped back in, the baby had stopped breathing. She picked the baby up and began to wail. Neighbors told her to bring the baby to Tata to find out who it was that killed the baby, because this was apparently not a natural death.

When Tata told her that it was the older woman who had touched her sleeping child that day, she took the dead baby home and told everyone she met on the way what had happened. A mob followed her to the house of the older woman. The older woman escaped, but the crowd set the house on fire. The older woman ran to the army barracks to alert her son, who had built her the house. Her son sent a detachment of soldiers to the family house. The soldiers came and took Tata away.

People began to talk on the street. Some of them were happy over the detention of Tata in the Army Cantonment by the soldiers.

—About time this came to an end. Witch this, witch that, everyone has become a witch since she brought her accursed mirror—

—The mirror has done more harm than good, brothers and sisters and family now view each other with suspicion. Even children view their parents with suspicion—

—When you give a child *akara* these days he'll tell you let me run home first and show it to my parents—

The soldiers who detained Tata said that at night they heard the sound of dashing waves pounding against the walls of her detention room, they said the place seemed to be floating. They eventually released her.

A few years later Tata became the founder of a church. Her followers wore white, flowing garments and each church had to be built near a flowing stream or river.

JULIUS

The Family House was in a festive mood. Brother Julius was returning home after many years abroad. If you asked any of us the name of the country he was returning from, we would have said to you that he was returning from a place called Abroad. Till today we do not know for sure what country he had lived in abroad, whether the United States, U.K., or in Germany or even Russia.

His return was marked by his anecdotes from almost every country in the Western hemisphere. According to Brother Julius, in Russia everything belongs to everybody, everyone shares. What is mine is yours. There was no private ownership of property. You entered the unlocked Lada car parked down the street with keys in the ignition, you do your errands; you leave the car keys in the car, and the next man who needs it picks it up. Share and share alike, everyone is happy. Everybody, including their president who was not called President but Comrade, lived in the same-size flat with the same type furnishings, he told us.

According to another of his stories, while we are waking up, the Australians are going to bed. Australia is the end of the world and the end of the earth. If you walk too far out on the Australian desert you'll walk off the edge of the earth and fall into another planet.

The British love tea and will drink tea when they are happy and drink tea when they are sad. They'll drink tea when they are hungry and when they are full. They love their cats and their dogs and all their pets. They have a society for the protection of animals and none for the protection of their fellow humans. They'll hug a tree to prevent it from being cut down but their ancestors sent debtors and their children to prison and would go to watch a prisoner being hanged and sit down for a picnic of sandwiches after the execution.

What was remembered most about the day he returned was that there was so many free soft drinks that we used our half-drunk soda drinks to wash our hands, like we did when Gramophone got married. We also ate so much fried lamb meat that there was a long line in front of the toilet the next day. He was Grandpa's favorite son; even our parents whispered that it was Grandpa that had spoiled him.

He had been sent abroad to study in the first place because it was said that the course of study he wanted to pursue was so complicated that no university in the continent offered it.

People needed no invitation to come and eat. There was more than enough food for everyone. After eating, the people on the street gathered to pick their teeth, belch, and talk.

—Now that the son has returned from abroad he will bring some civilization into the house—

—He should at least send those scary souls living in the house away. They scare everyone. I couldn't even take the food offered by one of them earlier today—

—He will change things, even from the way he speaks. If you were in the next room you'd think it's a foreigner speaking—

—What can he do? What will he change? Was it not the money from the house that sent him and kept him abroad all these years?—

—He should have gone to stay elsewhere if he was different. Since he returned to the same house he is part of it—

—Exactly what did he study abroad? Is he a doctor, lawyer, or engineer?—

—What did he spend all these years studying?—

—I hear that what he studied is so specialized that no university in our continent offers it—

—We are still here. We are not going anywhere. We are watching. We shall see—

The expectation of both Grandpa and every other member of the family was that Brother Julius would get a job, marry, buy a car, and move into his own house, but this didn't happen. Brother Julius had a different plan. Brother Julius wanted the party to continue and it did for days and days after his arrival. There was talk of a job but Brother Julius had everyone, including Grandpa, confused about what exactly he had studied in school and what could be done with his qualification. Someone said he had mentioned international criminology, but when he was asked if that meant he could join the police force he said that was very far from what he studied.

All of these things would not have been a major cause for concern. After all, people said that there was enough money in that house to feed all the people on that street for all the years of their lives. Trouble started when Brother Julius began to entertain the hairdresser popularly known as Man-Woman, who lived two streets away. A man, he was known all over the neighborhood for his feminine ways. He painted his long nails pink. He had his hair in Jheri curls. He preferred tight white trousers. He swayed his waist from side to side when he walked. He tied his towel on his chest and not on his waist on his way to the bathroom. He stood and gossiped with women all the time. And when the women said something funny he laughed in a tinkling manner and covered his mouth coyly with his fingers.

He was known to be generous, and even those who didn't like him had no reason to be hostile toward him. The womenfolk liked him and confided in him. He had the secrets of the menfolk in his hands. Initially it did not surprise anyone that Man-Woman came to the Family House to greet Brother Julius. The man had just returned from abroad and well-wishers were free to walk in and have a drink or even just to see the face of the returnee. The strange thing about the visit was that they hugged like long-lost brothers and had eyes only for each other, such that without being told other guests who were sipping soft drinks and White Horse whiskey, had to slip out of the room. When they left they heard the door shut behind them and then there were soft girlish giggles from Man-Woman. In the days that followed, Man-Woman began to bring different guests to the house. They ate, drank, talked, ate some more, drank tea, and laughed loudly. The only time Brother Julius said anything to anyone was in response to Grandpa's accusation that he was having an everlasting party and that no party lasts forever, when he told Grandpa that this was not a party but that he was holding a *salon* with his new friends.

—And what is this we hear that he has turned that house into a hotel for all kinds of people—

—He claims it is not a hotel but that he is holding a *salon*—

—What is that? Did he go abroad to learn hairdressing?—

—Don't we have enough barbing and hairdressing saloons on this street already?—

—Even Kafa calls himself a London-trained barber and his London-Style Barbing Saloon has been there since that boy was a kid—

—He says it is not that kind of saloon. His is a *salon*, a place where they gather to talk about ideas for the betterment of society—

—So why do they shut the door when they discuss these ideas?—

—You are asking me as if I've been in there with them. I am not a member—

—So tell me why is it that it is only people like Man-Woman who attend the meetings?—

—What society do they want to make better, they want to destroy the world that they met with their strange ways?—

—I heard that all those men who enter that room *follow their fellow men*. They go with their fellow men—

—Shhhh, hush, don't say that. This world is live and let live—

—But how do they make money from this *salon*?—

—They say the *salon* is not meant to make money, it is for the discussion of ideas for the betterment of society—

—If it does not make money, how can it better society?—

—You are asking me?—

—Who do you want me to ask; did you hear that I am a member of their secret *salon*?—

—If it is a secret society, that one is good. The secret society members help themselves. Once you give each other the secret handshake, it is like you are both born of the same mother. You will give the other person the shirt on your back—

—But who pays for all the drinks and food and tea that they consume in their meetings—

—They have money in that house. Money is not their problem. First I thought it was the man from abroad funding the thing but I hear he did not return with a single brass farthing—

—He keeps telling everyone that his things are still on the high seas, that he could not carry much with him on the flight—

—Well, all I can say is that if they cannot make the world better, let them not ruin the world, they had better leave it the way they met it—

The parties continued. Now, there was no longer anything furtive about them. They were having parties. They were playing loud music. Some people who said someone saw men holding the waist of other men and they were dancing *hold-tight* in there.

Grandpa finally summoned Brother Julius for a man-to-man talk. He asked him when his stuff would be arriving from abroad. Brother Julius responded that the shipping company said the goods may have been missing on the high seas or that the ship lost its route due to high winds but would be arriving at the ports soon.

What about getting a job? he was asked.

He said by the nature of what he studied he was more comfortable setting up a consultancy firm.

And what exactly had he studied that had no name or that was only mentioned in vague terms?

He was an expert in the area of international criminology.

Had he considered joining the state secret police? Force CID at police headquarters?

He was not in the same field as the secret police.

And then Grandpa, having circled the subject as much as he could, asked Brother Julius about what was bothering him most. It wasn't the issue of getting a job, that wasn't a problem at all. There was enough money in the house to feed generations to come. As Grandpa used to tell us, the difference between him and others was that he had planted a money tree in the Family House, which will continue to bear fruit into the future if not in perpetuity.

"People have been whispering about the company you keep. That all kinds of people come to the house. *Such and such* people. People they do not quite know how to describe. People that are neither birds that fly in the air nor four-legged animals that walk on land."

Brother Julius responded that he was a grown man and that he would keep the company of whoever he wanted.

Grandpa said he didn't have a problem with that, but it would be better if Brother Julius did what other grown men did, such as getting a good job and getting a car and driver and moving into their own flat, and if they wished, they could live the highlife lifestyle to the fullest by throwing a party every weekend or every day for that matter.

One of the surprising members of the *salon* was a married man named Seleto. He was a happy fellow, always smiling and buying people drinks in neighborhood bars. People wondered what he was doing with the *salon* crowd.

—He is probably there for the free drinks. He loves to drink with people—

—He can afford to buy his own drinks. He always offers to buy for people—

—He probably doesn't know what is going on there—

—Maybe they have initiated him, you can never be sure—

—You mean converted him?—

—It is like a club, when you join, then you become a member—

—I hear there are benefits of being a member. They say they can recognize themselves anywhere—

—They say a lot of important people are members and that they reward each other with jobs and contracts—

—I think Seleto and Julius were in high school together. He is just keeping the company of an old schoolmate—

One morning Seleto's wife ran into the Family House, screaming. She was dragging her husband with her. She screamed. She wailed. She cried. She cursed.

"What have you people done with my husband's manhood?"

"What did you use his manhood for?"

"Why have you people stolen the thing that makes him a man?"

"I warned him when he started coming to this house. I told him the house is evil. I told him that only bad stories ever came out of the house. I told him to start following other women, to get a girlfriend, but he would not listen. Was it the drinks in this house? My husband can buy his own drink and everyone knows that."

She started screaming one more time.

"Come outside, you, and give him back his thing." She was calling on Brother Julius.

"All the evil that you people have been doing in darkness I know it would come to light. Now it has come to light. Come and repair the damage you have done."

People had come out of their houses by this time and were looking at the house and listening to Seleto's wife.

—What did she say happened to her husband?—

—She said they took his manhood—

—How did they take it? Has it disappeared completely?—

—I do not know. Nobody has seen it—

—You remember a few years back there was the case of disappearing manhood—

—Oh yes I remember. We were warned to stop shaking other people's hands. First we were warned to stop shaking the hands of strangers and then later we were told to stop shaking the hands of anybody because it wasn't just strangers that were doing it—

Brother Julius came out and so did Grandpa. They were asking Seleto's wife to calm down and to stop screaming. They said that whatever the problem was, it could never be solved by screaming. They asked Seleto to say what happened, but Seleto pointed back at his wife.

"Since he began to come to this house to party every evening he has not been living with me as a husband should. He always complains that he is too tired or too drunk to do it. So this morning I got angry and threatened to leave him unless he agreed to do it with me only to discover that what made him a man is no longer there."

"Disappeared, how? How has it disappeared? Show us."

They looked around and drove the children away and asked Seleto to pull up his flowing djellaba.

Nobody was quite sure what they were going to see when he pulled it up. Was the place going to be flat or sealed off completely? How would he pee?

According to those who saw it, they said Seleto's manhood was still there but it had shrunk and was looking like it wanted to run back into wherever it originally emerged from.

—We thought you said it is gone but it is still there—they said to Seleto's wife.

"You look at it with your two eyes—does it look alive to you?"

—If it is dead, then you go wake it up. After all, you are his wife—

"It wasn't dead until he started coming here. That was when he stopped looking at me like a woman."

—You better leave if you do not want us to lock you up— she was told.

As we later heard, Grandpa called Brother Julius aside and asked him to go back overseas and promise never to come back, that he would have all his expenses taken care of. He agreed. He departed with none of the fanfare with which he had returned. He departed like a thief in the night.

Those who asked after him were told that he had been offered a job abroad because there was no company in the country that could retain the services of a specialist in international criminology like Brother Julius.

BABY

Baby lived in the Family House. Though she was older than us, we all called her Baby. Baby was not really a name as such. It was more of a placeholder. A baby born in the father's absence, perhaps the father was on a journey, was called Baby until the father returned from his trip, and then there would be a ceremony when the baby was properly christened with a proper name.

Baby was often described as behaving like someone who fell off a moving train. We sometimes saw overloaded trains with passengers hanging on the door and windows and some who were squatting on the roof hurtled down the rail tracks on its way to the terminal. To imagine someone falling off this train and surviving it was difficult to do, but anyone who did must have had their brains pretty shook up.

There were many stories about Baby. It was said that the reason she was banned from going to the major department store was because she was in the habit of quarreling with the mannequins.

"Am I not greeting you?" she was said to have said to one, and hissed.

"At least, if you do not have the courtesy to greet, you should have the courtesy to respond to people's greetings."

And when there was still no response from the mannequin she had called to a passerby and complained.

"See this lady, she would not greet me and when I greeted her, would not respond," she complained.

All outlandish deeds were attributed to her. She was said to have nearly killed a little baby in her care who was running a fever. She had tried to force the baby into Grandpa's Frigidaire. When she was accosted she had responded that it was not her fault. She had been told that items went into the freezer hot and emerged cold.

We played pranks on her. At night we would call her and ask her to blow out the flashlight the way you would blow out a flame. She would blow at the flashlight furiously and we would laugh at her.

One of Grandpa's favorite sayings is that no person is completely useless in this life. So he put Baby to use and made her try her hand at many things. She was first in the machete shop selling stuff, but she could not tell the difference between large and small bills. She would give customers change that was more than the amount paid. It was noticed that whenever she was the one in the store the place filled up quickly because those customers she had given change or undersold items to would tell others, who in turn would tell others that Baby was the one selling. After that experience she was soon sent to hawk iced water in cellophane packs. Each was sold for one naira so nobody could cheat her. She was told not to sell to anybody who did not have the exact amount.

Baby hawked sachets of cold water on a construction site to workers building an overhead bridge. The workers were mostly from neighboring foreign countries. They loved Baby because they could grope her as much as they wanted without any objections from her. She laughed at every action. She would sell two dozen sachets during lunch break and go back to the store and bring back more. They all paid her. No one tried to cheat her. As long as she was willing to be groped they were all happy. There was one guy who didn't grope her. He would talk with her and was satisfied even if all she did was grin. His name was Asare. He was also from one of the neighboring countries. He was a bricklayer but worked with the construction company as a laborer because it paid more. He talked to her about missing his country. He talked to her about how people here were always in a hurry, unlike in his own country. One day he told her to come back to the construction site when everyone had left. He took her behind a concrete mixer, lifted her dress, and entered her. He was quickly done. He gave her money and told her to dump all the unsold water sachets into the lagoon. She complied.

Three months later Baby wouldn't eat. She grew pale. Someone heard her retching in the toilet. She cried. Grandpa asked her who was responsible for the pregnancy. She said it was *Akwanumadede*. *Akwanumadede* was a popular highlife song from one of the neighboring countries, and most of the construction workers from there were nicknamed *Akwanumadede* by their counterparts. She was asked to take them to the worksite. By the time they got to the construction site, the bridge was already completed and the workers had dispersed.

There was a childless rich trader who owned lots of stores close to Grandpa's store. The rich trader's name was Janet. She was a big distributor of smoked catfish, which she bought cheaply from the North, where they had it in abundance, and sold at a profit. She had her own house, a two-story building with the legend LET THEM SAY written on the entrance. She loved gold and had gold rings on every finger and a massive gold chain and pendant on her neck. People greeted her politely but talked behind her back.

—With no child of her own when she's gone, who will she leave all her wealth to?—

—Her womb produces money, not children—

—In life some people choose before they are born between wealth and children—

—And why does one need to choose when it is possible to be blessed with both—

—Her relatives will share all her stuff when she is gone. They will even sell that castle of peace mansion—

Nobody knows whose idea it was, but between both of them it was agreed that Janet should marry Baby. She would also become the father of the child that was in Baby's womb when the child was born. Baby would live with her and would meet as many men as she wanted to, but any child she had in the process would be Janet's child.

There was some talk that money had changed hands. There was talk of the unborn baby having a price tag, but since no one was there when Janet and Grandpa met, these were mere rumors.

Though they were both women and this was said not to be a common practice, it was known to happen. Though we were not told this, a woman could marry another woman. Baby would live under Janet's roof and cook and wash and take care of Janet as a wife would. Baby was free to pick any man she wanted. The baby born out of such a relationship would belong to Janet. It was going to be a big event. Janet was the husband to be and was going to pay for food, music, and drinks.

On the street people whispered about the strange wedding of Baby to another woman.

—It has never happened before for a woman to marry another, some said. The world is coming to an end, strange things are happening—

—Surely, the world is coming to an end—

—Oh it has. It used to be quite commonplace but that was in the olden days—

—They are doing this to her because she behaves like someone that fell off the train. This is what they usually do with people like her—

—So much evil goes on in that house—

—I think they are helping her, otherwise who else is going to marry her—

Baby began to be treated with a lot of generosity and kindness. People in the house were warned to stop addressing her as Baby and start calling her by her new name, Patience. How the name was arrived at, nobody knew. It was not a baptismal name, but all agreed that patience was a virtue and that Baby had lots of it and would need tons of patience in her new role. She was given the choicest portions of food. She got some new nice clothes. She was encouraged to take a walk around the neighborhood to show off her new clothes and her new look. As she walked around on her stroll people congratulated her on her forthcoming wedding. Her response to every comment was a sheepish smile. Behind her back people whispered.

—If they had a chance in that house, they would turn human beings into goats just so they can sell them off for profit—

—That is the kind of house that sold people into slavery in days gone by—

—What do you mean in days gone by? How is what they are doing these days different from slavery?—

—She is even lucky. She may likely have an easier life with Janet than she has had in that evil house—

—So she is to have no choice; any man that comes she opens her legs—

—Not really. Some choose to settle for one man, have all their children through the one man so the children don't look too different from each other—

—That Baby that laughs at everything. She is never going to be able to choose. She'll accept whatever is thrown at her—

The event was planned to be grand. Baby was taken to the market to shop for new clothes. She was taken to have her hair braided in a beautiful style. She was encouraged to invite her friends, but alas poor Baby had no friends. It was the first time that the whole street was invited to a party in the Family House. Janet invited her fellow traders. It was assumed by some of them that a relative of hers was getting married.

It was during the dry season and everywhere was hot. Sheds were built. Big red-and-blue metal drums were filled with cold water, and drinks were packed into the water to keep them cool. Women were hired to fry beef and cook *jollof* rice and *moin-moin*.

—Not even for a proper marriage between man and woman have I seen such preparation—

—So much food being cooked, so many drinks being cooled—

—I heard they slaughtered two cows and countless chickens—

—I don't blame the woman, though. It is a terrible thing to come to this world and leave empty-handed with no one to answer your name when you are gone—

—But what about the poor girl? It is almost as if they are selling her off—

—It is not just her they are selling off, they are selling off the unborn baby as well—

—Well, as for me, I have never been known to reject free food—

—Me neither, not when they have free drinks thrown in as well—

—Be very careful what you eat in that house—

—Why, it is food cooked for the public? Don't tell me you think they'll poison everybody?—

—There are things worse than poison. And poison may be even better, because it kills you and that is the end—

—So what is worse than poison, eh, tell me?—

—What if after eating you turn to *mumu*, a doddering fool?—

—*Mumu* for what? For eating *jollof* and chicken?—

—Why do you think they are able to keep all the people who work for them acting like *mumu*?—

—Ah, one has to be careful, I tell you—

—Once it has gone into the mouth and the stomach, it is not coming out again and the damage is already done—

—I don't think they are that totally gone to try to turn all the invited guests to *mumu*—

—I think at worst you can call it appeasement. They are using the food as *sara*—

—Which wouldn't be a bad thing. They need forgiveness for all they have done—

There was not much to the ceremony. The only major thing done was that drink was poured into a glass cup. Baby was expected to look around at the invited guests and give the drink to her husband. She had been warned ahead of time not to embarrass the guests by giving the drink to Janet. She knelt down and gave the drink to a young man seated next to Janet who was also dressed in white. The young man took a sip and handed the glass back to her and she drank. A large box was handed to Grandpa's representatives. Some said it was filled with money, some said gifts. That was the end of the ceremony, now guests could go outside to eat and drink their fill. When Baby said she had a headache and was going inside to rest, people said it was not surprising. Her new hairstyle must have given her a headache. She should wash her face with cold water and rest for a while.

People ate and drank and some even took some food home in plastic bags. Many who attended invited those they met on the way.

—They are still serving food. No discrimination, everyone who shows up gets served—

The plan was that on the next day, Baby would be taken to her new husband's house. This would be done quietly and not with the usual fanfare that would accompany someone moving into a man's house. This would have required singing and dancing and another round of feasting.

Everyone on the street woke up to hear that Baby was gone. The bride had disappeared. She left. Who had seen her?

Apparently at some point that night Baby had disappeared from the Family House without taking anything with her. She had left no trace or clues behind. She had confided in no one. This was strange, that she had planned and executed her escape. Even though she was considered to be feeble-brained by all, it was a surprise. Coupled with the fact that the walls in the Family House were known by all to have cavernous ears.

—That boy from the neighboring country who owns the pregnancy must have come for her—

—And you won't believe this but she was all smiles yesterday, nobody knew what she was planning—

—Is there a time that she doesn't smile?—

—She must have decided not to exchange a harsh master for a harsh madam—

—Who knows? It may all be their plan. You know how they are in that house—

—So what is going to happen to all the money the woman spent on the ceremony?—

—What about the gifts and the box filled with money that she gave to them?—

—What about the things you can't see, like the shame she is going to suffer at the hands of her fellow traders?—

—Some people are destined not to have children. That is her destiny. She cannot wash it away no matter how much she tries—

—It is not an easy destiny to live with—

—Is this not the reason why it is called destiny? Good or bad, you have to accept it because destiny can never be changed—

—One thing I know was that the food was great and nobody is going to ask me to return what has already settled finely in my stomach—

—Mine has already been converted to proteins and vitamins in my body—

—As for me, all I can say is it serves them right. What kind of abomination is that? A woman being given in marriage to another woman—

It would be assumed that this would be the last we'd hear about Baby but it wasn't. Baby came back one day a few months later. Her skin scratched and with scabs in places. Her hair matted. Those who first saw her said she looked like a madwoman. Some said she looked like someone who had returned from the dead. And the story she told was that she had indeed come back from the dead.

Baby said that on the night of her wedding ceremony she had gone to the bathroom in order to wash her face to see if her headache would ease but discovered the bathroom was occupied, so she decided to take a bowl of water and go wash her face in the backyard. She said she scooped the water with her hands and was about to splash some on her face when she felt a hand tap her on the shoulder and a voice said *follow me*. This was the last thing she recalled. She said the next place she found herself was in a mud hut deep in the forest along with some other men and women. As she came to in the hut, a tall, dark giant handed her a piece of red cotton cloth and told her to undress and tie the cloth around her chest. The people around her were cowering, very scared, some were sweating, a few were muttering prayers or incantations, but she couldn't be sure. She heard someone say that they had been kidnapped and that they were going to be used for money rituals by having their heads cut off and their eyes gouged out and their breasts cut off. It was dark, they were all standing, at intervals the door of the hut would burst open and the giant with the lantern would come and grab someone and take them outside, never to return. And so Baby slept standing, waiting for them to come and grab her. Her headache was completely forgotten.

The next night the giant came for Baby. She had been given nothing to eat since her capture but she didn't feel hungry. They took her to another hut. There was a giant carved pot-bellied statue covered with blood. There was a juju priest with a fly whisk. He touched Baby's head with the whisk. Baby shuddered more out of the fact that the whisk felt ticklish. He touched her breasts; he touched her belly and jumped back.

"Why did you bring this one to me? Can't you see she is already with child? And besides she is incomplete. She is not a complete human being. Take her away from here and get me a complete human being."

Baby was taken away. When she got back to the hut, those who were standing in the hut touched her and asked her, What happened? How come you came back? Why did they bring you back? And they shrank back as they asked her these questions because none who left had ever returned.

She did not know how long she stayed in that hut. She couldn't quite recall if she ate or drank. All she remembered was that one day they released her. She was taken a ways from the hut by the giant and after walking some distance in the forest was given a shove on the head and told to move along and not to look back and never to come back.

She said she wandered in the forest for a long time. When asked how long she wandered in the forest she would say for a long time. Numbers had never been her strong suit. Eventually she ran into a hunter who asked her what she was searching for so deep in the forest and she responded that she was lost. When asked where she came from, she responded that she lived in the Family House. The hunter said he knew where the Family House was and brought her back home. She was asked where the hunter was so that he could be thanked for saving her life but she said the hunter had simply dropped her off and left.

—Have you heard the story the bride who scampered on her wedding night is telling?—

—She says she was captured and kidnapped by ritual killers but had managed to escape. She told another person that the ritual killers let her go because only people who had all their faculties intact could be used for rituals. She was rejected by the gods—

—She had to come up with a story that would be more fantastic than a woman marrying another woman—

—She sometimes acts as if she is not *complete, not all there*, she is not the type that would make up stories—

—Why, but she was smart enough to escape on the night of her marriage—

—Don't be fooled, I know her type. She at least knows where to put it when she is doing the thing with a man, or does she put it in her nose?—

—We have heard of some people putting it in places more peculiar than the ears. And in that house too—

When Baby was asked what happened to the baby in her womb she said she didn't know. At what point did she notice the pregnancy was no longer there? she was asked.

"One day the pregnancy was there and then the next day I looked at my belly and the pregnancy was no longer there."

Baby had gone back to being her old inarticulate self, who talked like someone who fell off the train.

There was talk of meeting with Janet and returning her gifts and money to her, but Janet sent word that they could keep it. She said she was happy that the marriage hadn't worked out and that she was sure Baby would have given birth to children that were not complete human beings, since she was not a complete human being herself.

OLUKA

O f all the things that were said about the house, this was the
one thing that was considered the factor that led to its fall—
the death of a child. No one could say for sure that they saw it
happen but it was like the smoke before the fire. As the saying
goes—the owl cried last night and the child died in the morning,
who can deny that the owl had a hand in the child's demise?

Quite a few people are of the view that this was the worst
thing that had ever happened not only on the street or in the
country, but the worst thing that had ever happened anywhere
since the world was created, in fact in the history of mankind
on this good earth.

Uncle Oluka was one of Grandpa's older sons. He was
quite successful and had his hand in many businesses,

including a block-making factory. He was married to a very beautiful lady we all called Miss because she was a school-teacher by profession. Miss did not have a child. When we were brought to the Family House over the long summer holidays, Uncle Oluka and Miss would come around too, but since they had no children of their own to leave behind in the Family House, a certain silence and quietness seemed to follow them around. Yet Miss was very generous and loved children. She always had a gift for all the kids in the house, a piece of candy here, a coloring book there, a stick of red chalk. What I remember most about her was that she left a faint trace of her cologne on everything she touched. Her cologne smelled like carnations.

Still there were those who did not want to see any good-ness in her kindness. They said spiteful things behind her back and even within her earshot.

—How can two men be living in the same house? A woman that cannot bear children is no better than a barren fruit tree. What do you do to a barren fruit tree? You cut it down with an ax and use its wood for firewood—

—Why is the man struggling to acquire all that wealth? Who is he going to leave it to when he dies? Why work so hard when you have no heir to inherit all the wealth you'll leave behind you when you die—

—You know what they do in my place to such women? They send them packing; they throw their stuff outside the house and sweep away their footprints with a broom so that they can take their aridness along with them—

—Don't forget she is someone's daughter? It is not her fault—

—Are we not saying the same thing? She is someone's daughter; that is the main reason we are asking that she in turn should be someone's mother. The same way her mother gave birth to her is the same way she should give birth to someone too—

—But that is not even the worst thing about this whole shameful story. The most shameful part of it is that she has never had a miscarriage, not even one, so we can say she tried but it is not her fault or that she is going to have another one—

—And the poor husband always makes his own clothes from the same fabric as his wife. Is it "and co" they call it, or is it "me and my wife," I have forgotten the name—

—Ah, you people, God will judge you people one day—

And then Miss became pregnant. For a long time she had not been to the Family House, and when she turned up, she was many months gone and her belly was protruding heavily.

Soon, the story was all over the street and the same tongues who had excoriated her could not say enough good things about her patience and how her pregnancy was a testimony to God's everlasting faithfulness and mercy and kindness.

—God is not sleeping—

—It would have been a grave injustice on the part of nature for them not to have children. Such a beautiful couple. They are made to produce beautiful children—

—She loves children too. She always distributes sweets and biscuits to all the children on the street. You know

God listens to the unspoken prayers of children because they are so innocent—

—Not only that, unborn children select kind couples to have as parents. Children oftentimes choose the homes they want to be born into—

—But you have to give it to the husband too. He is a real upright guy. All these years he withstood the pressure to marry a second wife, not once did he consider throwing her out of the house. People talked a lot and called her all sorts of names—

—It is the way of the world. No matter what you do, people must talk. Have lots of children, they'll say uncountable children, uncountable troubles. Have none, they'll say you are selfish. No matter what you do, people must talk; it is the way of the world—

And then Miss had the baby, a boy. At birth the baby would not cry. The midwife was confused for a moment, and then she lifted the child up high with one hand and spanked the newborn baby's pink bottom, which was still smeared with blood, three times in quick succession. It was only then the baby sputtered a weak cough and then whimpered feebly.

"All babies cry when they are born because they are leaving their more peaceful world into this our chaotic and wicked world of ours," the midwife said.

Miss was weak and tired and was happy that the baby had come out at last after a long and painful labor. She was not bothered by the baby's not crying. All she wanted was to rest and for people to hear that she had given birth to a child.

"Well, if you don't want to cry, you can at least laugh," the midwife said, and began to tickle the baby. The baby made no movement but shut his eyes even tighter.

Almost everything was hard for the baby to do. He found it difficult to suck, difficult to fasten his slack lips around the mother's nipple. Difficulty with stooling and even when he managed to stool, it came out in little pellets like goat shit. He would not drink water. He would not sleep at night. Initially it was speculated he was still living in womb time and had yet to adjust to earth time. He did not open his eyes, and when he eventually did, would look at neither his mother nor any person but had his eyes focused on the ceiling.

"Every child is different," the midwife said. "Some come into the world on their head, some enter with both feet, and some even want to arrive this world sideways, with their bodies aslant in their mothers' womb. Some cry a lot, some play a lot, some neither cry much nor play much and grow up to be thinkers. I suspect your son is going to be a thinker one day."

And then the child began to cry. As soon as he discovered the joy of crying he took to it like a champion. Not only did he cry, but he seemed to relish it and would stretch taut both feet and both hands as he cried. He cried when he was being given a bath, he cried when he was feeding, he cried when he was held, and cried when he was put in bed. Even when he slept, he slept fitfully and would sniffle and smother a cry even in his sleep.

Miss was unhappy and her eyes rimmed red from lack of sleep and worry, but her husband had never been happier.

"Remember what someone once said to me? You have been married now for many years and we have not even once heard the cry of a baby from your house. I am happy because the cry of a baby can now be heard from my house at all times," he said.

But soon he too began to worry. Eating was difficult for the baby and so was keeping down his food. When they tried to make the baby burp, he simply vomited up everything he had been fed.

The child was named Amaechi—who knows what the future holds.

And as it turned out, one never knew with Amaechi.

He could not sit, he could not stand, and he could not lie on his belly or lie on his back. He had no food preferences, he loved neither water nor breast milk or powdered milk. He slept in the daytime albeit fitfully and cried through the night.

Uncle Oluka began what would turn out to be an almost endless consultation with doctors to find out what was wrong with Amaechi. They did scans and X-rays and tested his urine, his poop, his saliva, and even his sweat but found nothing wrong with him.

They consulted a native doctor. The native doctor told them to bring a white ram and a black ram, a white cock and a black hen, they did.

The native doctor took the child from the mother and tickled him, the child did not smile or show any sign of being tickled, the native doctor turned the child over and spanked him lightly on the buttocks, the child did not scream but whimpered lightly.

"This one does not want to be here. This one is not meant for this earth. He was forced to come here and wants to return from where he came. His days here won't be long, you'll see."

They took Amaechi to a priest of a white garment church, Baba Aladura. The priest closed his eyes.

The priest hummed a tuneless song.

The priest spun around on both legs like a dervish,

The priest shook and shivered like one with a fever.

The priest began to sweat and wipe fat drops of sweat off his brow.

Finally, the priest spoke in a whistling singsong voice that sounded like a whisper.

"It is not good to force the hand of God. There is a difference between God's will and the perfect will of God. When a beggar asks you for alms and you are reluctant to give, you give the beggar your alms in the worst possible way. When you force the hand of God, he gives you, but not a perfect gift. We shall bathe this one for seven days and seven nights in the Atlantic Ocean."

It was done.

Nothing changed.

Amaechi was taken to the university hospital. They ran tests. They X-rayed his bones. They took urine samples. They took stool samples. They found nothing.

No one quite remembers who it was that said it to the couple or if the couple came to this decision themselves. The voice said to them—*Kill this child before this child kills you.* Amaechi was brought to the Family House and it was done.

How was the child killed?

Was a pillow placed on his face and used to suffocate him?

Was the child placed facedown in a basin of water and drowned?

Was the child physically strangled with bare hands?

No one knows for sure except the person who did it. The only thing the relieved parents were told was that the child died without putting up a struggle. He did not struggle one bit. He was happy to go.

People said that the couple should adopt a child after their ordeal with Amaechi, but others countered that an adopted child would never be considered a full member of the family. The couple did not listen to anyone. First their visits to the Family House became few and far between, then they finally stopped coming.

GABRIEL

Gabriel was considered the unluckiest person on earth. After his string of misfortunes his relations told him to come and live in the Family House, perhaps his luck would change if he lived under a lucky roof. Gabriel started out as a farmer. He planted yams and a few other crops. He wanted to be a rich man. He said his ambition was to own a house with twenty-four rooms. He didn't prosper as a farmer of yams. His yam harvest was usually poor. One year his harvest was good and he built a barn for his yams. He was proud of his yams. He boasted he would sell them and start work on his twenty-four-room house. That year there was a mysterious fire. Gabriel's barn caught fire and most of the yams got burned. He invited people to come with palm oil stew to the farm and eat free roasted yam. How much roasted yam could people eat?

The next year Gabriel planted tomatoes. He had gone to a nearby village to learn how to grow tomatoes. He said he was going to buy a pickup truck from the proceeds of his first tomatoes when he sold his first harvest. He said he would supply a manufacturing company the fresh tomatoes they needed for the manufacturing of their tomato puree. After he had planted the tomatoes, just before they would start ripening, a strange worm attacked the tomatoes. They shrank, they changed color, and they rotted and began to stink. That was how Gabriel's tomato-planting adventure ended.

Gabriel decided to move in a totally new direction and went into the lumber business. Lots of people in the business were switching from handheld saws to motor saws. With the handheld saw, cutting down a tree was a lot of work. First the men had to dig a long trench into which the tree would hopefully fall, and then two men clad only in underwear would hold the saw from two ends and start sawing away. It took weeks for the tree to fall, though they lucked out sometimes when the tree was only half-cut and then there was a storm.

Now someone had invented a motor saw that could fell trees within minutes and actually cut them up into manageable flat small parts. The popular brand was Dolmar. Gabriel's plan was to get a loan from the cooperative society and buy one of the new machines and then hire a sawyer to operate the machine. He would transport the timber to the big city and sell it off there. He got the loan from the cooperative society and bought the motor saw. He called friends to celebrate the purchase of the motor saw. He boasted that he was soon going to become a millionaire. He said this motor saw was going to be the first of many more to come. That although this was his first, he would soon buy more. He also said he was going to buy a lorry with an iron body that would be transporting the logs to the big city for him and then he said that there was nothing stopping him from having his own timber shed in the big city. He said he could even start exporting his product to America, where he heard that even the rich built their houses with wood.

The man whom Gabriel hired to operate the new chain saw was nicknamed Sawyer; no one recalled what his real name was anymore. He was dark, a bit squat, and had really big muscular arms. He was adept at using the handsaw and would sing as he sawed, sweating heavily and ignoring the midges and tsetse flies that sucked away on his sweat and blood. He had not been trained to use a chain saw but said he would read the manual overnight. He did read the manual and used the saw to cut off a small tree to the admiration of onlookers. Some noticed that his hands shook and that the powerful machine seemed to want to jump off his hands but he gripped it firmly. He was a strong man.

That night Gabriel threw a party. He invited people to come and eat and drink. He bought the drinks with the remainder of the money that he had borrowed from the cooperative society. He was in a boastful mood. He said that this was just the beginning of great strides in business and once again drew a map of some of the things he planned to do and how he was going to expand his business and export timber to

America. People drank and danced, including Sawyer. A few whispered that they hoped Gabriel's luck would change, because behind his back Gabriel was nicknamed the man with the shit touch—everything he touched turned to shit.

Sawyer set out early for the forest with an assistant and the chain saw on his shoulders. The assistant carried a half gallon of gasoline. They first cleared around the tree with a machete, then Sawyer started the chain saw. It jumped into life and this startled Sawyer but he held the engine firmly in both hands and began to cut into the huge *iroko* tree. The trouble with the new machine was that it cut so far into the trunk quickly and he could not quite gauge the direction in which the tree was leaning. He cut and jumped back, and shielded his eyes from the sun's glare as he looked to see the direction in which the tree was tilting but he was not successful. Although it was only midday, Sawyer told his assistant that they should go home. He hoped that there could be an overnight storm that would help fell the tree.

When Sawyer came back so early, even without asking him, Gabriel was already boasting to people that the new saw could fell a dozen trees in a day. Sawyer explained to him that he decided to come back early so he could consult the manual but that he was sure the next day he would have mastered the saw.

Early the next day, Sawyer's assistant was screaming and panting as he ran into the community. He had apparently run all the way from the forest, where they were felling the timber.

"Sawyer, the tree fell on him. He is under the tree. Him and motor saw."

—Who is asking you about motor saw? Is his waist broken? Or his legs? Or his hands?—

"All of him is underneath the felled tree."

—Oh, no, was he screaming when you were coming?—

"I could not see him. He was under the fallen tree. I could not help."

The men gathered themselves together, including Gabriel. It took a lot of effort to roll the fallen tree aside. The Sawyer was dead and buried forcefully into the soft earth. The motor saw was smashed to smithereens, with pieces scattered all over. Even the rock-hard white end of the spark plug was ground up finely.

The sawyer's family came for their son's body. They also came with a long list of things Gabriel should buy before they could bury their son. A white cow, seven black chickens, seven white chickens, seven yards of Hollandaise Dutch wax cloth, kola nuts, six bottles of aromatic schnapps, a bag of rice, and the money to marry a bride for their dead son who had never married. If all of these were not purchased, their son would not be buried, but even if he was buried his spirit would not be at rest and would haunt Gabriel and pull him into the neither-living-nor-dead world, where the spirit was now wandering.

Gabriel borrowed more money, some of his relatives contributed, they pleaded with the sawyer's family to tamp down their demand. Finally, the family agreed. They reduced their demand. Instead of aromatic schnapps they accepted a bottle of local gin *ogogoro*. The sawyer was buried.

Gabriel did not rest, he was soon embarking on another business venture. He had met a man called Adamu who was a cocoa buyer. Adamu supplied dried cocoa to the manufacturers of cocoa drinks and chocolate makers. So he claimed. He appointed Gabriel his buyer. Gabriel's job was to buy from the local farmers on Adamu's behalf and Adamu would pay Gabriel a commission. Adamu drove a big Honda 175 motorcycle.

—Won't he give up? Is it not apparent to him that wealth is not in the stars for him?—

—Why does he keep struggling, you cannot change destiny—

—Some people never learn, if he had been left alone and no one came to his help the other time with the sawyer case, he probably would be dead by now—

—I don't blame him, life is a struggle. The day you give up struggling is the day you die—

—If I were him I'd stop and ask myself why I am the only one who never finds success—

—He boasts too much, that is his problem. He was already boasting of how he would build a three-story house even before the first tree was felled by the motor saw—

—It is not good to boast, sometimes one's boasting falls into the wrong ears—

Gabriel was given a bicycle by Adamu. It was not free. It was on loan, and the full cost was going to be deducted from Gabriel's commission. Gabriel was proud of his new bicycle and the smell of the woven bags with which he was to collect the cocoa. Even when he fell from the bicycle he boasted that it was better to fall from a bicycle than to fall while walking on foot. A younger cousin of Gabriel's had the job of driving away greedy goats from the cocoa spread out to dry properly while his friends played soccer.

Adamu soon came and picked up the bags of cocoa collected from different individuals by Gabriel. When Gabriel asked for payment, Adamu said to him not to worry. He would sell to the companies that buy the cocoa and then he would come back to pay. That was the last that was heard from Adamu. Even the bicycle, Gabriel soon discovered, had been bought on credit and was soon repossessed by the seller. Creditors flocked to Gabriel's house. They wanted their money back. Even those from the cooperative threatened to send him to prison.

—Why doesn't he go and try his luck somewhere else?—

—Can't he see that as long as he remains here he will never make any progress in life?—

—The forces holding him down are more than the eyes can see—

—He will just kill himself or be killed by those dragging him over money owed—

—His best bet would be to move to the house of his distant relation—

—You mean the man who owns the Family House?—

—Yes, his luck would definitely change there—

—If you live under the roof of a lucky man and his shadow falls over you, that may erase all the years of bad luck—

—To tell you how lucky the owner of the Family House is, everything that is planted around the house multiplies and bears so much fruit that the fruits weigh down the trees. Even the chickens and dogs and cats in that house multiply. Everything they sell, even water, sells out fast. It is a lucky house—

—The story I heard is different. They say he takes the luck of all those living under his roof—

—What I heard is that he uses their life to extend his own life—

—Gabriel is better off anywhere but here at any rate, his creditors will drag him to an early grave—

One morning Gabriel arrived at the Family House, presumably leaving his bad luck behind and hoping to start afresh.

He was soon going to the shop to help sell. He offloaded machetes from the truck. He helped wrap them in cement paper. He helped arrange them according to their different designs, sizes, and shapes. He was learning. He was happy. He was already thinking of how one day he would own his own store. He was thinking of how he would have a machete-loaning scheme for farmers who would then give him half of the harvest at the end of the year.

One day Gabriel was walking back to the Family House when he saw something a dull golden color on the ground. He picked it up. It was an empty bullet shell. He put it in his pocket and continued walking home. When he was lying down in his corner at night he brought it out of his pocket and began to polish it with a piece of soft cotton cloth. As he continued to polish it the color began to change, it was now glowing. This became his pastime every time he was in bed. He loved the way it felt in his hand. He loved the way it responded to the cotton cloth. He would put it in his pocket all day and would only bring it out when he was lying in bed.

Gabriel was on his way back to the Family House when he heard running footsteps approaching. People were shoving him out of the way. Some people fell, stood up, and continued to run. Some lost their balance but regained it and continued to run. Gabriel did not see any reason to run. He was as a matter of fact fascinated. There was always one spectacle or another in the city. This was going to give him something to reflect on and chuckle about when he lay down later that night, polishing his toy.

"Hey you, don't move. Don't move one inch," a voice commanded.

Gabriel could not imagine that these words were meant for him. He continued to watch people who were fleeing. They now seemed far away. They were no longer running. They looked like small objects in the distance, but he could see them looking back nervously.

Two strong arms gripped him. He was startled. He turned around. They were armed policemen. They were chasing a thief or a robber, it was not clear but they were after someone. Now they had him.

Gabriel did not return home. Nobody knew where he was. He was arrested and searched. The shiny empty bullet casing was found in his pocket. There was no need to ask him any further questions. He was taken straight to prison.

By the time he was eventually released he had lost a lot of weight. He was told to remain in the Family House and see a doctor but he refused. He preferred to return to the village.

People in the Family House said his case was like that of the man who was visited by death. Death showed him a list of names, your name is top of my list I must kill you today. Unknown to death, this man made the best-tasting yam pottage. Don't kill me until you have tasted my pottage, the man pleaded. Death agreed. After all, Death reasoned, I will still kill him today whether on an empty stomach or on a full belly and why not do it on a full belly. The man went and prepared the most delicious yam pottage for Death. Even the aroma made Death's mouth water. The man served Death the yam pottage in beautiful dinnerware. Death was taken aback by the man's act of hospitality, nowhere had he been this welcome or well received. Death enjoyed the food so much that after eating, Death decided to take a nap. As soon as Death began to snore, the man went to Death's list and moved his name from the top of the list to the bottom. Death soon woke up, stretched, and decided that he was going to do the man a favor and repay the kind host for the hospitality. Death decided that instead of starting from the top of the list, he would start at the bottom.

Until this day people still say that if living in the Family House could not cure Gabriel of his bad luck, nothing on earth could.

CURRENCY

Uncle Currency, according to what we heard, had the best job in the world—his job was burning money. His job was to throw bundles of old, torn, discontinued currency notes into a huge furnace. He spent money the way others drank water. People said, how do you expect him to treat money with any respect, when he burned money every day? We heard that he entered his workplace wearing only his underwear and emerged wearing the same so that he would not have the opportunity of pocketing some of the money headed to the incinerator. But he was soon bringing bundles of currency into the Family House. How did he do it?

The bundles of currency were not new, in fact some did look tattered and torn, but money was money, and they could be Scotch-taped and repaired. Some looked moldy and even smelled, but it was the smell of money and you could always give them a bath. It was from him that we first saw money being given a bath. He would fill a large basin with clean water. Powdered detergent was poured into the water and the old currency was poured into the soapy water and stirred around gently. The water was poured away and then the currency was rinsed. The money was taken indoors and placed on an ironing board, and white paper placed between the board and the money and then the currency was ironed. It emerged crisp and ready to be spent.

Currency was said to be a model worker, or so we heard initially. He always had a stack of shiny coins on the table in his room. Things began to change when he started coming back to the Family House with a large bag that looked like a postman's carrier bag.

Initially he would go to work in the mornings and come back later in the evening, but soon we were told that he was now working what was referred to in quiet tones as *permanent night duty.*

We were expected to tiptoe around his room when we were passing by it because he was on permanent night. Either he had just come back from work and was tired and sleeping or he was sleeping before he left for work.

We would later hear that it was during night duty that Currency and his colleagues and the policemen and soldiers who were the security guards at the mint came together and held a meeting.

—How can we be burning money when it is what we work for?—

—We don't even have enough of it and we are burning it—

—But we must show that we are doing our work—

—We can burn something, it doesn't have to be money—

—We can burn newspapers and other forms of paper—

—How do we do this without anybody finding out?—

—We are all in this together and, come to think of it, we are not doing anything wrong, we are merely helping—

—I agree we are helping; it is like eating food that is going to be thrown away regardless—

Soon we heard in the Family House that there was an underground building being constructed outback. Everyone referred to it as underground until the bricklayer, a man nicknamed Puei who always had a menthol cigarette burning on his dark lips, told us it wasn't an underground building but a basement. It was in this new basement that Currency was piling up the money he was bringing in from work. Initially he and his colleagues had been operating on the principle that if they stole too much the owner would notice, so they burned half of the money and kept half, but soon enough they were not even burning any at all. They were now burning ordinary paper and taking all the money for themselves.

Evidence of the money coming into the house was everywhere. The house was repainted in white and there was even a suggestion that it should now be called the Whitehouse, but someone mentioned that another Whitehouse was already in existence in a far-off country. A new borehole was dug and a water pumping machine installed. New electrical fixtures were installed. New carpets were laid. Even the old wire mosquito nettings on the windows that had turned tobacco brown from dust exposure were replaced. And of course these changes did not go unnoticed.

—Have you heard the latest? The son is bringing money to the house in bags—

—Money in bags? That must be juju money. Only the banks have enough money to carry in bags—

—He works at the security mint where they print money—

—I know someone else who works there, it doesn't mean they can take the money as they please—

—He works in the incinerator. He works at the place where they burn the money—

—Ah, so it is money that should be burned that he is bringing home—

—That is a big one, but how does he do it?—

—He is not alone. They have people at the top—

—I don't blame them, though, why burn money. This money that is so scarce that we poor people never have enough—

—If you ask me, I think they should find a new way of disposing of the money. Why burn it? Why not just give it to the poor?—

Soon rumors began to circulate about money that should be burned finding its way back into circulation. Someone later attributed the leak to one of the people in the team who had bought a used car and had a sign boldly painted on the back windscreen that proclaimed: MONEY HAS NO MASTER. Others said it was because of the lavish lifestyle of some of those in the team. When confronted, a certain one among them had said that money was like smoke—it could not be hidden.

One night Uncle Currency and his colleagues were arrested while on night duty. They were caught red-handed stuffing bales of cement paper into the furnace while another member of their team stuffed old currency into a van. They were first taken to the office of head of security for questioning.

"Tell me everything and we'll make it easy for you," the head of security said to the men in the team, who were all wearing only white briefs, as they were all expected to not wear anything with pockets while working.

"Tell me, how long has this been going on?"

The men were silent. They had all agreed that if and when this day eventually came, they were all going to swallow their tongues and not utter a word.

"Keeping silent will not help you. We just need to be sure the money has not fallen into the wrong hands."

Still the men were silent.

"You know every piece of currency has a number. This means we can trace the money, and anybody caught spending it will be arrested. We do not number the money for nothing."

The men remained silent because deep down they knew the security manager was lying; they had spent some of the money and nobody had noticed any difference, the money had simply done what they were told money did best, which was to circulate—it had gone back into circulation.

The long and the short of it was that the case died. The men in the team were asked to resign. They were told never to say a word to anyone as to the reason why they lost their jobs. They were told to keep whatever it was they had stolen and to never step foot in the mint again, they should not even return to visit their former colleagues. Those who heard said that the men told the security supervisor that they would share their loot with him and he let them get off slightly. Others said that it was because the men in the team had enough money to consult the best native doctor and the best Aladura Prophets and this helped them to get away with their crime. Whatever it was, Uncle Currency was now without a job. He told those who would listen that he had amassed enough money to pay himself a pension even if he lived as long as Methuselah.

One morning we woke up and Uncle Currency's posters were on walls and electric poles and on trees and empty drums and on house gates and on corner shops and roadside stalls. He was contesting for elections as a councilor. The man who was the present councilor had been a councilor for so long that many assumed that his name was councilor. He had never faced a challenger, and when he heard that Uncle Currency was contesting against him he sent emissaries to him to ask that Uncle Currency withdraw from the race.

"Wait until I die, I am not greedy. I am not the type that will say I want my son to be a councilor because I am councilor. You are still young. Wait until I pass away in office and then you can take over."

People on the street wondered why Uncle Currency was going into politics to contest as an ordinary councilor.

—Why doesn't he want to stay home and start enjoying his money?—

—Why does he want to waste his stolen wealth on politics?—

—He should go and contest for something bigger and leave the old councilor to continue—

—He is not happy that he is not in prison for theft—

—Why are you complaining, this is the only chance we have to get our hands on that money. Let him contest. At least he'll spend that money and some of it will get into our hands—

—Do you want to vote him in, the council doesn't have enough money for him to steal—

The councilor soon sent a delegation to Grandpa to tell Uncle Currency to forget about his ambition for now and wait for the councilor to serve out his term.

"He is not a child, he is a grown man. I cannot tell him what to do."

"You can at least advise him to wait his turn. I waited my turn. That is the way we met it, it is the better way."

"I think he has his mind made up. There is nothing I can do."

"At least you can help me inform him that a young man may have more clothes than an old man but he cannot have as many rags."

It was assumed that no one would be attracted to Currency's campaign, but they were wrong. Early the next morning women brought out large iron pots, bags of rice, vegetable oil, and tomatoes, and a cow was slaughtered. As the aroma of *jollof* rice rose into the air and spread into nostrils, people began to gather in front of the Family House. It was free food.

You need not bring anything but yourself. The food was free, served in a plate and a spoon provided. It was like a party. After the feasting people were told to spread the word, the slogan was OUT WITH THE OLD AND IN WITH THE NEW.

When the old councilor heard the slogan they said he cursed aloud, saying those who are singing *out with the old*, may they never grow old, may they never taste old age, may they perish young.

Soon, though, the slogan was in people's mouths, and was being shouted from street to street. It began to crop up in regular conversation between people. If a man bought a new shirt and his friend observed that he had a new shirt on he would tell his friend that we now live in an age of out with the old and in with the new. If a man had a new girl-friend, he would say that he was following the new slogan to get rid of the old and bring in the new.

The cooking and sharing of food continued. It was a party every day. In the morning people gathered and sat on iron chairs while waiting for the food to be ready. As soon as the food was ready there was no need to line up to be served; the food was brought to them right where they were sitting.

Three days before the election Uncle Currency disappeared. Better put, he vanished. People saw him in the morning going from door to door, then they didn't see him again. Kidnapping was out of the question, no one kidnapped a grown man in broad daylight.

Tata Mirror was consulted. She said all that her mirror showed to her was that he was going to return. People were sent out to search for him. The next day his posters were mysteriously pulled down from trees and electric poles and walls and iron gates. People who came for their free food were sent away. They were told to join the search party.

A delegation was sent to the old councilor to find out if he had anything to do with Currency's disappearance. His response was to raise his palms outward and upward. Everyone knows that I have always played politics with clean hands. I know nothing about this and I will be vindicated.

By the day of the election, Currency's candidacy was already forgotten in keeping with the saying that you cannot give a man a haircut in his absence. People went in and voted. They came out smiling and saying to no one in particular that it wasn't their fault that the other candidate decided to abscond, if perhaps he was around they would have voted for him because they had not forgotten the free food he gave to them.

Just before the election the old councilor came up with a new slogan—New Is Good but Experienced Is Better. When asked if he knew anything about his missing opponent, he gave the same response, showed his hands, spread them out, raised them heavenward, and answered—my hands are clean.

—We all know how he made his money—

—You cannot start with evil and end up with good—

—Like the old councilor said, life is turn by turn, you wait your turn in life—

—Good things come to those who wait—

—In our generation the saying was that the patient dog gets the bone but for this generation they believe the patient dog starves to death—

—At least he shared his money by giving food to the masses—

—What is food, you eat it today and you shit it out the next day. The old councilor brought pipe-borne water to our neighborhood—

—Sad, though, no one deserves that fate, better to be dead and buried than to disappear and give false hope—

And then one morning a few days after the election, Currency wandered back into the Family House. He looked like he had not slept or had a bath for days. He could not say a word. He simply stared at everyone. He couldn't respond to any questions.

He was given a bath, his clothes changed. He was given a haircut. The next morning he took up a position that he would occupy for the rest of his life. He pulled a wooden chair and sat on the balcony overlooking the street and began to count from one to five thousand, after which he would start from one . . . He would occasionally dip a finger on his tongue, as if to moisten the finger, then commence counting all over again.

When he was called inside to eat he would go in and eat. He spoke no words to anyone. He gave the impression of someone who did not understand words. But when he started his counting there was a serene, satisfied look on his face and he actually articulated the words out aloud. Because of this it was at least known that he still had the ability to speak. But for the numbers, he said no other words and made no other sounds. He showed no interest in the people around him.

People did talk about the man who sat on the balcony of the Family House counting numbers. Children on their way to school would watch him as his lips moved, wondering if the numbers coming out of his mouth were the same as the ones their teachers wrote on the blackboard in school.

—But this world is bad simply because he wanted to be a councilor, an ordinary councilor, look at the high price he had to pay—

—He should have just continued to enjoy his money and leave politics for those who know how to play it—

—How do you know it was the old councilor that did it to him?—

—That is true, I never heard anybody accuse the old councilor of being that evil—

—You know he got a lot of money when he worked at the place where they print money. They even had to build an underground house for the money—

—So what are you suggesting? You think they did this to him because of his money?—

—I am not saying anything, don't ask me questions to which I have no answers—

—There is nothing they will not do in that house for money—

—You should rephrase that to say: there is nothing they have not done in that house because of money—

And so Currency sat from day to day on that wooden chair on the balcony of the Family House counting away one . . . two . . . three . . .

SOJA

We all called him Soja, a corruption of the word *soldier*. We heard that when Soja was much younger and only a member of the Boy Scouts he was already using his Boy Scouts uniform to intimidate bus conductors and avoid paying his bus fare. It was no surprise when he absconded from school in form two and took the train to the army depot up north to train as a soldier.

Later when he returned from training wearing his well-starched army uniform and gleaming black boots, he regaled listeners with stories of his time at the training camp. He said one of the duties of fresh recruits was to sweep the nearby military cemetery where all recruits who died in training and the soldiers who died in local and foreign wars were buried.

He said the sergeant-major who was their training instructor would bark at them to sweep the graves thoroughly. He told the fresh recruits that they'd be buried there sooner or later. Sooner if they died during their training or later if they died on the battlefront. You have sold your body and soul to the army and we can do with it what we like. Among other things, the sergeant-major told them that the first soldiers were bandits.

He made them stand on their heads for any infraction. Soja had a bump at the center of his head when he returned and he proudly showed this off. He said the weaker recruits had a small square piece cut from their foam mattresses that they slipped under their head when they were asked to stand on their heads.

He said time and again the sergeant-major asked them to repeat and chant the motto of the training camp. They all shouted—*There Is No Going Back*. Yes, there is no going back for you. If you die here we bury you here. If you run away, better kill yourself because if we catch you, we'll kill you. They frog-jumped them, they belly-crawled them through razor-sharp barbed-wire fence; they made them do push-ups until they felt they were doing push-ups even in their sleep.

They took them into the bush and made them practice shooting at one another with live bullets. The sergeant-major boasted that one trainee soldier died during training for each of the twelve years that he had been training army recruits. He said this was the thirteenth year, and because thirteen was an unlucky number he was hoping that at least two or more recruits would die in training instead of one.

Soja later said that his time at the training camp was the best time in his life. He said that what the country needed was a sergeant-major to drill all citizens every morning and everyone would fall in line and the country would be shipshape.

Soja was discharged from the camp with the rank of *korofo*. Meaning that he had no rope but he was a soldier and had his uniform, his beret, and his boots. What he told people when he came back from training was that every soldier was given a shot annually. It was this shot that made soldiers superhuman. He said that every soldier was given an ampoule of liquid bravery. That was what the shot was; it was pale, like the color of blood. He said after the shot the soldier had a mild fever and then woke up feeling as strong as stone.

Soja's first job was with the Environmental Task Force. Their job was to ensure that everywhere was clean. Streets swept, gutters and drains cleared, ensure there was no street trading. They patrolled streets and markets and roads and looked along the rail tracks for those who broke the law by selling their goods there. The task force was made up of soldiers, a few naval personnel, and an air force corporal. They drove around in a dark blue Toyota Hilux truck.

Initially people commended them for the good job they were doing. They made tenants and landlords sweep clean their gutters, cleared drains, and swept streets. They made street traders leave the streets, which helped the flow of traffic. They ensured that everyone stayed home and cleaned their homes on special days designated for cleaning and sanitation. But all these soon got old.

It was not long before Soja started bringing home baskets of produce, used coats and pants and dresses. The task force now carried out raids. They would swoop in on unsuspecting street traders, brandish their guns, chase them away with a *koboko*, and throw their goods into the Toyota Hilux truck. They would sometimes throw the traders in with the seized goods, drive with them a little ways, dispossess them of the money in their pocket, and then throw them out of the truck, meanwhile not returning the seized goods to them. Every day Soja brought different types of goods to the Family House. The edible things like chicken, tomatoes, pepper, and other foodstuffs were consumed in the house. The other items like clothes and sometimes electronic equipment were sold off. The traders would sometimes be made to buy back their own products. The task force was actually supposed to charge repeat offenders to the Environmental Tribunal set up for this purpose, but they didn't.

—What they are doing is worse than armed robbery—

—They are stealing with authority backing, it is pure authority stealing—

—Does it mean no one can stop them?—

—I thought the work of soldiers was to go to war and fight; now they are waging war against hardworking traders—

—This is their time *jare*, let them enjoy it. After all, life is turn by turn; it may be your turn tomorrow—

—It will never be my turn to steal—

—It is always from that house that all things both good and bad emerge—

—Can you imagine the poor traders being forced to pay twice for their own goods? They have to buy back their seized stuff—

—This is why the price of goods continues to go up, and they always go up and never come down—

—I hear the task force members gather to share money and goods like robbers after a successful robbery operation gathering to share their loot—

—People are now lobbying to join the task force but initially people called them glorified sanitary inspectors, ordinary *wole wole*—

—They have the support of the authorities who are higher up—

—They make returns to the big *Oga*'s every day—

—Ah, in spite of all the money they have in that house, they are still collecting from the sweat of the poor—

—Is that not what they specialize in? One day is one day, the monkey will visit the market one more time and will not make it back—

—Is it monkey that they say in the proverb or the baboon?—

—Monkey or baboon, what does it matter? It will for sure not return from the market—

People complained that before the government could ban street trading or clear the street of roadside traders they should provide shops and build more market stalls. Soja and his colleagues in the task force were no longer interested in charging those they arrested to the tribunal. In some cases they were not even interested in letting the trader pay a bribe to get their goods back. They were not interested because they were opening their own stores and selling all kinds of dry goods. When they seized or confiscated enough DVDs they opened a DVD store; if they seized enough children's wear they opened a shop to sell these. The fear of the task force was the beginning of wisdom. Traders in the major markets supported members of the task force. They said roadside and street traders ruined their business because they had no overheads and could therefore sell their stuff at a cheaper rate.

And then one day Soja fell sick. He could not empty his bowels for seven days. He was given lots of oranges and grapes to eat to *soften* his belly. At intervals he'd be led to the specially made toilet in the backyard and asked to try and push.

—Try. Try harder. Push as if you are having a baby—

"I am pushing," he would respond through clenched teeth.

Nothing happened. His eyes became muddy colored. He said he had no strength. He walked like a man with a heavy weight attached to his waist.

—We said it that one day the chicken would come home to roost—

—Look at him now is he not the one suffering—

—What punishment can be worse than not being able to pass stool?—

—It is the spirit of all the poor people they deprived of their means of livelihood that is now haunting them—

—Think of all the curses that were rained down on them when they confiscated innocent traders' goods—

—What made it worse was that they even began selling off the goods and opening their own stores—

—They must have offended someone whom they shouldn't have offended—

—That is true. There are people who must not be offended—

And then Soja began to use the toilet and could not stop going. He went so many times and had the urge to go so much that he sat on a wooden bench by the door of the toilet.

It would be assumed that Tata Mirror would have been able to find a cure for Soja's illness, but Tata said that if a person did you no harm and you decided to harm them, then if the victim in their anger decides to place a curse on you, no god or goddess will come to your aid. She said that Soja had offended a very old woman whose only means of livelihood was going to the bush market to buy tomatoes directly from farmers, which she later sold at a profit. She said that she sold tomatoes along the railway tracks because she was too poor to rent a stall in the market. She said that on the day Soja and the members of his task force had seized her tomatoes, she had begged them but they had refused, that what stung her was the fact that she had called Soja her son—help me, my son, she had cried, but Soja had pushed her away and actually whipped her with his *koboko*. As the members of the task force drove away with her basket of tomatoes, she wept. According to what Tata said, the woman had woken up at midnight and had taken off all her clothes and had placed a curse on Soja and his task force colleagues.

All through these events Soja's wife had decided to take him to a white garment church for healing. The members of the white garment churches wore no shoes because they believed that all the earth was a holy ground. They wore only white garments as a proclamation of their holiness. They drummed and danced and fell into trances and saw visions. They proclaimed all kinds of fast—white fasting in which they ate only white things like pap, milk, white bread; dry fasting, in which they ate nothing at all; and sweet fasting, when they ate only honey. They had special feast days, too, on which they killed rams and sheep and cooked *jollof* rice and drank warm soda. Soja's wife had benefited from his being a member of the task force. She used to be a trader herself and had actually had her goods seized, which was how she had met Soja and moved in with him. She had opened a small store where she sold some of the stuff that was gotten from the raids on traders.

—Did we not say it?—

—Are they not the ones running from herbalist to native doctor to white garment church now?—

—We said it then that they were stealing from the poor, hardworking traders who were only struggling for their daily bread—

—Even the special injection they give to soldiers could not save him from this illness—

—They said that for seven days he could not pass stool—

—And seven days later he started passing stool and could not stop—

—They should go and beg all those poor market women and men that they stole from—

—Even the wife has closed down her store—

—No more confiscated goods; what is she going to sell in the store—

—Was she not confiscated herself? How did they meet? She was one of the traders helping her mom, whose goods were confiscated. She was thrown into the task force truck. That was how she met him. She followed him back and began living with him—

—Their eyes have not started to see *pepper*. Very soon they'll be consulting *Alaafa*—

Soja had lost a lot of weight, and with his shaven head and his emaciated body in the flowing white garment he took to wearing, he looked like the angel of death. He was told to wear the white flowing soutane at all times because it would make his body the temple of God and death should have no dominion over it.

Instead of Soja getting better, he developed boils and rashes all over his skin. There were tiny boils where his eyelashes used to be, one boil for each eyelash. He had rashes on his skin. The head of the prayer band at the white garment church where he was being looked after said he should be taken to the world headquarters of the church so that his spiritual leader could say the word and Soja would be healed.

It was hard to get ahold of the spiritual leader because there was usually a long line of people waiting to see him. They said all he did was utter a word or phrase and the supplicant's problem would be solved. To a woman crying because of her sick child he could say *cry no more your tears will become tears of joy.* This would mean that the child would be healed.

He would say to a spinster *you will no longer walk alone,* meaning she would soon get married. Cryptic phrases that were assiduously recorded by a bearded acolyte called the Scribe. He took down every word and utterance, coughs, and sighs of the spiritual leader.

Invoking esprit de corps with the policemen who served as guards for the spiritual leader, Soja and his wife were able to jump to the front of the line and see the spiritual leader, who said to Soja—*I release you to your destiny.* Even the Scribe could not interpret the expression. What was Soja's destiny? Was his destiny to live or to die? They left more confused than before. Soja's wife decided to take him to an Islamic sheikh who was reputed to heal by dipping his prayer beads into water and giving the water to the supplicant.

—Have you heard what I heard?—

—They say the spiritual leader of the white garment church could not heal him—

—I hear that man is powerful. If he could not help, there may be no hope—

—He sure is powerful. He eats no meat. Fasts for forty days and nights without touching any food—

—If the problem is one that he cannot solve, then the man should return home, put his affairs in order, and start waiting for death—

—His wife is still carrying him about from one healer to the other—

—I hear she has taken him to the powerful gray-bearded sheikh, the Islamic preacher and healer—

—I hear those ones are powerful too. They use words from their holy books—

—He has really suffered. Look at him, all bones—

The first thing that was demanded of Soja before he could see the sheikh was that he needed to convert, he should change his name and shave his hair.

He wanted to argue with them but they explained to him that it was all one God. He was only called by a different name. He agreed. His new name was Ahmed. He was happy. He covered his head with a *taj*, a cap worn by the Muslim faithful.

Finally he got to meet the sheikh. The sheikh shook his hands and touched his right hand to his heart in the Muslim fashion and said to Soja/Ahmed—*Inna lillahi Wa inna ilaihi Rajioon*. What the sheikh said to him was the Islamic prayer for the dead.

Grandpa said Soja's wife should stop carrying him from place to place. He said Soja knew what was wrong with him. He should say the truth.

After this people began to speculate about Soja's illness and the cause.

—You know when he was in the task force some of the female roadside traders bribed them—

—Of course everyone knows that they collected bribes—

—No, not that kind of bribe you are thinking about—

—The women who they took to their head office the task force head office you know—

—You mean they did things to the women?—

—Some of the women used what they had to bribe the task force people and get their goods back and free themselves—

—They got a lot of it, some members as time went on even preferred to be bribed that way. They say Soja was that way—

—Probably, that is what is killing him now?—

—Was it that he did it with another man's wife?—

—Not sure—

—If it was the one people got from doing it with another man's wife, the victim will fall off the woman, crow three times like a cock, and die—

—So if it wasn't that one what was it?—

—You won't hear it from my mouth. You know what it is that is killing him—

Soja finally died. They say he refused to go quietly. They said he died fighting. He struggled, he rolled from one side of the bed to the floor, he sweated, his labored breathing could be heard about three houses away. And then he stopped breathing. He was finally at rest.

Soja was buried in the military cemetery. Because of the speculation that whatever had made him sick was a result of his task force duties, his colleagues rallied, they contributed money for him and tried to get his gratuity and payment out very quickly. They were planning to give the money to the wife, but it turned out she was not the next of kin. Soja had never officially married her. Grandpa was the next of kin. He was the one who got all the money except for the contributions and the gratuity. Soja's woman cried, she begged, she threatened, she cajoled.

Grandpa asked only one question—she should receive the payment in her capacity as what?

Soja's woman did what she had heard the old woman did

to her husband. At midnight she stood in front of the house, bared her buttocks at the house, and cursed the house and those who lived in it.

She later repented and came back to beg Grandpa when she discovered that she was pregnant with the late Soja's child. Grandpa gave her a small space in front of the Family House where she could fry and sell bean cakes.

FUEBI

S oja's wife, who now had a daughter named Fuebi, was using the small corner outside the Family House given to her by Grandpa to sell *akara* fried bean cakes. It was a good location to sell *akara* because of the many feet that passed by the house. Her mother fried the *akara* in hot oil while Fuebi wrapped the hot balls in newspapers for customers. Beside them on a tray were loaves of bread, which they also sold. Beside the loaves of bread lay a pile of old newspapers. One of Grandpa's acts of kindness was to allow them to make use of the space in front of the Family House to sell. Fuebi's mother may have been beautiful many years ago, but she was now the same ochre-white color as the smoke that emerged from the cheap firewood with which she fried her *akara*. Fuebi was beautiful. She sparkled. She had a gap on her upper incisor, which was considered a mark of beauty. She had dimples. Her skin glowed. She smiled a lot. This was despite the hard work she had to do every day. Frying *akara* was the final task in a very laborious process that began with soaking the black-eyed peas in water overnight and washing off the tough skin the next morning. Washing and rinsing and pouring the water into an open drain very far from the house because the smell from the bean water was awful. Then carrying the washed beans to the communal grinding machine store where she joined the line to have the beans blended, then returning home to go to school. Coming back from school to go buy firewood and going to broad Teacher's place to collect old copies of the *Daily Times*. It was a tough job, but Fuebi never complained. She was always smiling. During a pause in sales or on days when due to rainfall the sales and frying came to a halt, the woman would turn to Fuebi and point at herself.

"Fuebi, hmmm, you must not let your life be like mine. Look at me, stained and faded like an old piece of cloth. How much do we make from all this suffering? From morning till night, fetch water, grind beans, grind pepper, cut onions, haul wood, build a fire, blow the fire, sit by hot fire and hot oil, all for what? All for a profit of a half a penny, all for penny and half penny. Your life must not be like mine. You must not allow suffering to steal your beauty the way it stole mine. Any slightest opportunity you get you better start running far away from here, far away from all this suffering. Suffering and beauty are not friends, and never will be."

"You are too hard on yourself," Fuebi would say to her.

"What do you know? You are not a child anymore. You had better open your ears and listen very well to what I am telling you. The day you have the opportunity to run away to where suffering cannot reach you with her evil claws, run and run very far away."

"Things can only get better, don't worry."

"Before our own very eyes things are getting worse. Look at me, eh, just look at me. If not for the death of your father, I know this is not where I would be. Death has done its worst. The good die young."

And then, one evening the answer to her prayers. Fide, the patent medicine dealer, pulled up in his car and asked to be sold some *akara*. Fuebi remembered the song that wafted from the car's speakers—it was "You're My Best Friend" by Don Williams. She would learn later that this was the only kind of music that Fide played. Fide called it sentimental music.

"I don't play with my sentimental songs," he would say to her when they got to know each other better. Fuebi would never forget this song because it was also the song to which he would insist on fucking her without protection, insisting he wanted her skin to skin, which would eventually lead to her pregnancy. But all that was in the future. This night he wanted *akara*. Fuebi's mother wrapped a generous quantity of *akara* for him and told Fuebi to go give it to the man in the car. She could smell the air freshener in the car from where she sat. By the light of the car, Fide looked at the beautiful gap-toothed face handing him the *akara* and he smiled and switched off the engine of the car. He brought out his wallet, protuberant, bloated, and overloaded almost to spilling with cash. He searched for the largest denomination and gave it to her. She went to bring back his change.

"Keep the change," he said to her, and winked, and then he smiled at her and drove away slowly, trailed by the smell of his air freshener and the voice of Don Williams.

When Fuebi showed the change the man in the car had left for her to her mother, she stood up and danced wordlessly around the fire and the pot of boiling oil on the fire. After dancing she poured water to put out the fire and said they should go home.

"What about the customers who want to buy *akara*?" Fuebi asked.

"Give the *akara* in the basket to them but do not collect any money from them," she said.

"But why are we closing so early tonight?" Fuebi asked.

"We are closing early because what I saw while sitting on this chair that I sit on every day to fry *akara* is indeed very marvelous in my sight," she said, and broke into a Pentecostal church song.

"And what did you see?"

"You mean you did not see how that man was looking at you?"

"He was smiling and he told me to keep the change."

"I can tell you today that things are not going to be the

same for us again. Soon, you will see, I will no longer need to roast myself on the fire in the name of frying *akara*," she said, and began to pack her things. "Mark my words, you'll see, this is not the last time we will see him."

She was right. The next evening he was back. His car stereo was playing Don Williams. He shut off the engine of the car and asked for *akara*. Fuebi went to hand the *akara* to him. Again the fat wallet appeared. Again, he handed her the fat denomination. Again, he asked her to keep the change.

That night when they got home, Fuebi was given a lesson by her mother.

"It is true you are young but you were not born yester night. The ripe orange fruit that refuses to fall off the tree to be eaten by a good man soon becomes food for the birds. That man likes you. He has shown that he likes you. Now, it is your turn to reciprocate, show him that you like him before he turns away. Men do not have lots of patience and are not good at waiting."

The next evening Fuebi not only took the *akara* to Fide, but she also sat in the car with him and asked him how his day went.

"Fine, my day always goes well. Honor to Jesus, adoration to Mary," he said, fingering the rosary that dangled from the rearview mirror.

"What do you do?" she asked.

"I do buying and selling."

"What do you sell?"

"I sell medicines, capsules, tablets. You know, like Panadol."

"That is nice," she responded.

"Do you take medicines?"

"I never fall sick," Fuebi said.

"I will come and take you out tomorrow evening."

"I don't know. I'll have to ask my mother."

"Don't worry. She is a good woman. I am sure she will say yes. Give her this envelope. Tell her it is from me."

Fuebi felt the envelope. It was filled with money. As she made to alight from the car, Fide drew her closer.

"Please stop, people are watching us."

"That is true. I will take you to someplace with fewer eyes next time."

When Fuebi handed the envelope to her mother, she sang and danced and said that indeed there was a good God in heaven who answered the prayers of the poor and sent them kind people to save them.

The next day Fuebi dressed up in her best, which was not much, and waited for Fide near where her mother sold akara. He pulled up, looked around, and told her to get into the car quickly. His manner was abrupt and he did not smile until they pulled out of the street.

"Like you said, there are too many eyes watching. One has to be careful."

He turned to her and told her she looked beautiful. He asked her if she was hungry. She said she was not hungry. He soon pulled up to a hotel and parked his car. The people at the reception seemed to know him very well and he took her up to a room upstairs.

"This is a good place for us to relax, away from all those eyes," he said.

She sat on a chair beside the bed and began to open the pages of a green Gideon's Bible by the side of the bed.

"Come and relax with me here on the bed. I am not going to bite you."

She joined him on the bed, and he wasted no time undressing her. As he took off her clothes he emitted a deep gurgling sound that seemed to emerge from some deep part of his throat. All the while he kept saying to her, you are beautiful, I am not going to bite you. With some force he pushed her legs apart and entered her. She felt a sharp pain. One moment he was in her and the next moment he was out. He looked down at her legs.

"This is your first time." It was a statement; not a question.

She nodded.

"You are a good girl, you are a very good girl and I will reward you." Once again he brought out two fat envelopes and gave them to her. "One for you and one for your mother."

Fuebi felt a little dull pain and throbbing below.

"Don't worry, the pain will soon go. If you feel any more pain, take two tablets of paracetamol. You'll feel better."

He dropped her off by the road near where her mother fried *akara* and drove off.

When she got home she gave both envelopes to her mother. Her mother opened them and began to dance around their room.

She told her mother that she was feeling a little tired.

"Don't worry. I'll boil you some warm water so you can take your bath and go to bed."

She took her bath and went to bed and was soon deeply asleep.

Twice a week, Fide showed up and took her to the same hotel. He seemed to take less and less time, after which he fell into a short sleep and snored, then would jerk up suddenly awake and tell her to get dressed, that he had some urgent business to settle in his store.

When Fuebi began to look pale and vomit in the mornings, her mother said that this was another answered prayer.

"Your father's spirit is too strong. I know he has been itching to come back to this world that he left abruptly due to bad people. See, now he is going to come back through you. And you have found a good man too."

When Fuebi told Fide her good news, Fide was angry.

"What do you take me for? Do you think I am an irresponsible man?"

"But what do you want me to do?"

"I am not the person who will tell you what to do. You are not a child. You know what to do."

"I don't know what to do."

"In that case, ask your mother, she will know where to take you."

"She says I should tell you, that you'll be happy."

"And what about my wife? And what about my daughters, will they be happy? And what about my reverend father, will he be happy?"

It was the first time Fide had ever mentioned a wife and children.

The next time Fuebi went to the store to wait for Fide, she spent the better part of the day waiting. She was told he had gone to the port to see to the release of his imported goods. When he came in and saw her his face changed.

"Take this note," he said as he scribbled something on the back of his card.

"Take this," he said, giving her an envelope.

He then directed her to go and see a doctor who would take care of her.

When Fuebi showed the note to her mother, her mother took the card with the scribbled note from her and said she was going to keep it as evidence. As for the money in the envelope, she said it was going to be used for baby clothes.

Fuebi eventually gave birth to twins. Two boys. The boys screamed lustily into the world. They were ravenous and began to eat as if they had been starving for the nine months that they had been in the womb.

"Look at their mouths, look at those greedy lips, just like their father's," Fuebi's mother said.

Fuebi was tired and was lying weakly on the bed. She had not seen Fide since the last time he gave her the money to go see his friend to take care of the pregnancy.

Word soon got to Grandpa that Fuebi had delivered a set of twins and that their father had refused to show up. Grandpa summoned Fide.

"What is this I hear about you refusing to see your God-given children?"

"It is not me, it is my wife. She will kill me. She has two

girls for me, two girls *only*. She doesn't want to hear that another woman had children for me."

"Are you a man or are you a woman who pees from behind?"

"And the priest will not be happy about it too."

"Were you thinking of the priest when you were doing it with her?"

Fide shook his head from side to side and began making squiggles on the ground with his big toe.

"Tell your wife that children bring children. She will see, as soon as these twins are under your roof, she too will give birth to her own male children."

And that was how it was settled. Fuebi moved into Fide's house. Just as Grandpa had said, Fide's older wife gave birth to a boy exactly one year later.

TRUDY

Uncle Zorro returned from his studies abroad with a white woman as his wife. This was great news and there was a big party to welcome him and the wife. But when the wife, Trudy that was her name, said they were not going to have children, that was when the trouble started. Trudy had started making enemies of most people in the house when she began complaining about the treatment of the cats and dogs. She was the one who had insisted that they live in the Family House and not in the posh expatriate quarters, where they could have gotten one of the more opulent houses.

The cats and dogs were working animals and were not considered ornamental or solely pets. They could be petted on occasion when they did a good job, but such occasions were few and far between. The job of the cats was to keep the house mice-free. There were many corners and dark crevices in the house. Tiny rooms, closets, and pantries where all kinds of odds and ends were stored were good breeding grounds for mice. We were told not to feed the cats with food or they would lose their hunting skills and become lazy.

All the dogs went by the name Simple. Simple was the original name of the mother dog. All her offspring were also called Simple. There was brown Simple and black Simple and black-and-white Simple. They all worked. They kept the house secure at night by barking and attacking any would-be intruder. They went hunting with Grandpa. They were also expected to play with the children.

Trudy complained that the animals were not well treated; she carried the cats around and would feed them by hand. Soon enough the cats lost interest in hunting mice.

And what was this about the need to plant flowers around the house? She said that it was a big shame that a house as big as the Family House did not have a garden, she said it was uncivilized and a disgrace.

There was a *dogonyaro* tree behind the house. Everyone knew that the boiled bitter leaf of the tree was a good cure for malaria fever. The limber stalk of the tree was a very good medicinal chewing stick and kept stomach troubles at bay. The tree provided shade under which we played when the sun became too hot. There was an orange tree and an avocado pear tree. There were no plantain trees because we all knew they were breeding places for mosquitoes. There were useful flowers like queen of the night, which kept witches and evil people away with its pungent, cloying smell. But Trudy wanted a real garden.

"And are you going to plant things in your garden that people can actually eat?"

"Beauty is the whole point. It must not be about food all the time. We must also feed our eyes, and our brains need to be fed sometimes."

She was given a space to start her garden.

"She is not from here. She must be treated with extra kindness," Grandpa said. "If she left her father and mother and family and crossed the vast ocean to follow you here, then you must do all that you can to make her comfortable."

Trudy soon turned her attention to the way the children in the house were treated. She felt they were sometimes treated in a cruel manner.

In the meantime her husband, Uncle Zorro, was already working in the general hospital as a doctor and was assuring us that she would soon drop her foreign ways and adjust to living life the way we all lived it in the Family House.

She said that the house was a breeding ground for germs and that she was surprised we had not all perished from all kinds of germ-borne diseases.

A few people who knew about such things said Trudy was not going to last.

—The ones who stay learn our language. They eat our food. They wear our traditional clothes. They genuflect when they greet their elders—

—They get pregnant and have many children, not carrying a cat around like a baby the way this one does—

And then the news began to filter into the house that Uncle Zorro had a concubine. Nobody used the word *girlfriend*, because this was too light a word to describe the relationship. A girlfriend was someone seen occasionally. The case here was different. Uncle Zorro would drive directly from work at the hospital to his concubine's house, where he would eat his dinner, read a newspaper, and take a nap before coming back home long past midnight. It was even worse than that, he actually went over during his lunch break or his concubine would send over one of her girls to deliver his lunch to him.

And it was not just lunch; he was blatant about the affair. His car was usually prominently parked in front of his concubine's house, where every passerby could see it. He was said to have taken over the payment of the fees of some of his concubine's children from a previous marriage.

They had been seen at parties dressed in "and co"—they had on identical clothes—and when they both stood up to dance the musician had referred to the concubine as the wife of the world-famous London-trained doctor who could tell what ailed you merely by looking at your face.

As usual, people talked about this. As usual, they blamed the white wife.

—Man shall not live by bread and tea alone. Even the holy book said so. What is tea for breakfast, tea for lunch, and tea for dinner? The tongue of a black person will always crave pepper. Or was it not a piece of spicy alligator pepper and salt that were dropped on his tongue when he was being given a name on the seventh day?—

—But if it is pepper that he craves, can't he get a native cook and steward like his other colleagues who are married to foreigners?—

—It is the fault of his wife. She is the mother of cats and dogs. Tell me what man wants to be known as the father of cats and dogs?—

—But couldn't he have gone about it more discreetly? How come he is carrying on like he is the first man to have a concubine? Men have been having concubines since the beginning of the world—

—It is the nature of man to easily get bored with the taste of one soup. Man wants to sample a different soup from time to time. So, even if the man was married to a woman, from her he will still stray—

—He had better be careful, though. I hear his wife's people do not hesitate to shoot men who cheat on them—

—Where is she going to get the gun from?—

—They always carry their own gun, not your long-mouthed double-barreled gun; their own gun is so small it can fit into their purse—

—He had better watch out, then—

—But what does he see in that *secondhand* woman who already has three children for someone else?—

—Who are you to question another man's taste?—

Trudy had at this point started going from house to house with an interpreter to talk to the women. She said she was talking to them about safety issues, teaching them to keep themselves and their surroundings clean. Teaching them about things that'll make them better wives. But this was not the report that was received.

—She wants to convert our wives to her white ways. She will not succeed—

—What does she know about keeping a man? If she knew anything about keeping her man, would he be keeping a concubine?—

—My own wife told me with her mouth that the woman told her that she was the owner of her own body and that as such I her husband could not touch her without her permission—

—It is possible that her own husband got tired of asking for her permission like a schoolboy and decided to go to a woman whom he doesn't need to ask for permission—

—I hear some of the foolish women are listening to her. Maybe by the time their husbands drive them away she will marry them herself—

—How will that shock us? Is there anything that they'll not do in that house?—

Nobody knew for sure if Grandpa had heard about Uncle Zorro and his concubine. Of course, even a newborn child knew that Grandpa knew and heard everything. A day came when Uncle Zorro came to talk to Grandpa about marrying his concubine. He wanted to bring her into the Family House. Not just her but also her three children from her previous marriage. Grandpa was furious.

"This your wife, Trudy, that followed you all the way from across the seas, I have a question for you concerning her. Where are her parents?"

"Her parents are in their country."

"And where are her brothers and sisters?"

"They are also in their country."

"So she has no family here except you."

"None."

"So did you bring her all the way here in order to abandon her and cast her away like a piece of rag?"

"But she is not adapting."

"You are the one who has refused to adapt," Grandpa said. "Look at you, you say you are the educated person, but you have not shown any sign that your so-called education has had any impact on you. You cannot even hide the fact that you have a concubine from the eyes of the world, or are you the first? I must not hear that nonsense about bringing some other woman into this house again."

Grandpa could still roar when he wanted to and his bite was even more dangerous. Uncle Zorro prostrated and promised to reorder his steps.

But Grandpa was not done with him yet.

"You must not step foot in that woman's house again. I forbid you to have any further contact with her. You must not meet with her, not even secretly. If anybody sees your car parked in front of her house again you'll see what will happen to you. Behave the way young men your age behave."

"But the woman I have at home has no child."

"And I thought you said you were a medical doctor. If she doesn't have a child, is that not your problem? Don't you treat women who have no children in the hospital where you work?"

"But she doesn't even want to hear about it."

"Am I the one that will teach you how to marry your wife? Were you born yesterday? Anyway, the most important thing is that your foolish concubine business is over."

How this conversation filtered down to the ears of those outside the house, no one knows, but they did hear. And as usual they had their views.

—I hear he stood up for the woman—

—He even warned his son to stay away from the infamous concubine—

—If only he acts like this all the time the house will not have such a bad reputation—

—He spoke up for her. Truly, she journeyed over seas and mountains and ocean to come over here with him. Why would he treat her that way?—

As if Trudy had also heard what happened she too began to change her ways. She changed her name from Trudy to Tunu. She began to wear only traditional cotton dresses and head ties. She also established what would later become famous as the Infants Home School. In the morning when the bigger kids had gone off to school she would go from house to house picking up the smaller preschoolers. She insisted that they be bathed and ready; she would go from house to house picking up the kids, who would be singing and marching behind her.

Oftentimes mispronouncing the words of the song but singing loftily all the same.

> *Today is bright and bright and gay oh happy day a day of joy*
> *Today is bright and bright and gay oh happy day of joy.*

They would march to the Family House and she would
spend the day with them singing and dancing and playing
games. She persuaded her husband to informally consult
when he came back from work in the evenings. And within
a short time she could speak our local language like a native.

AKWETE

Akwete was his nickname. The nickname had eclipsed his
real name so much that hardly anyone recalled what his real
name had been. His nickname was derived from his signature
call as he pedaled into a street with bundles of clothing fabrics
piled on top of each other on his carrier and some more piled
on the handlebars. He sold every type of fabric—George, En-
glish wax, Hollandaise, Abada, and even Jubilee women's head
tie fabrics. Children loved him; women loved him; husbands not
so much. He persuaded women to buy his clothes no matter how
little money they had. The cloth becomes yours as soon as you
make a penny down payment. I'll write your name on it and keep
it for you. The day you make your last payment I hand it to you.
With that he persuaded the most reluctant women to buy from

him. Akwete, children would scream, imitating his signature call.

After he had done selling he would come to the Family House to chat with Grandpa. He grew from being a bicycle owner to the owner of a Honda motorcycle and eventually bought a Peugeot pickup truck. When he was not selling clothes, traveling up and down to buy clothes or collect money from his customers, he loved to hunt. He had a double-barreled hunting rifle. He enjoyed hunting and told interesting hunting stories.

He said that every animal had a peculiar smell. He said that as a good hunter what he always did was to bury his nose in the belly of every animal he killed, that way, the animal's peculiar smell became encoded in his memory. The next time he went hunting, he could tell if that type of animal was in that particular bush. The moment he entered a forest to hunt, he would immediately exclaim, I smell an antelope, I smell a deer, I smell a wild boar.

Some people had unflattering things to say about him. He was a man who was ever smiling, as if he had discovered the secret of happiness as soon as he was born.

—What kind of man sells women's clothes?—

—Why does he not sell men's clothes?—

—What manner of man is always comfortable sitting around with women, haggling with them, sharing their jokes and letting women touch him?—

Whenever Akwete came to Grandfather's house and these words got to his ears, he would laugh and utter a couple of aphorisms.

"Even the money made from packing poop smells as sweet, money has no gender, let them say what they like, nobody can please the world."

Even his hunting exploits gave them something to talk about. For he was also a good hunter and would sometimes kill a wild boar and sell it for lots of money.

—How did he even become a hunter?—

—I never heard that he learned to hunt from anybody. We know that every hunter's father and grandfather were also hunters. Where or who did he learn his own hunting from?—

—One morning, he went to the market and bought a double-barreled gun and went into the forest and shot his first deer and brought it home—

—Does that story sound right to you, he was not even afraid of going into the forest alone at night?—

—What I hear is that some people have a talisman that turns them invisible in the forest and that way they can hunt and kill all those animals without the animals smelling them or hearing them approach—

To these comments Akwete simply replied that those who were interested in knowing about his skills as a hunter should go with him into the forest at night or should transform themselves into a herd of wild boar and see if he would not gun all of them down to the last animal. All these negative comments did not stop him from always smiling and joking with women and persuading them to make a down payment on his cloth fabrics with only a penny, just a penny, he would say again and again for emphasis, all the while laughing.

Akwete went hunting with this friend of his, a school-teacher named Joachim. It was not the first time they were hunting together. It was a moonless night and they both wore miner's lamps on their heads. They turned the lamp on when they heard the sound of an animal; they would temporarily blind the animal with the dazzling light and then shoot.

Akwete and Joachim separated and said they'd meet under a designated tree later on. Everyone knew Akwete hunted alone, which was why he had all the stories swirling around him. When Akwete narrated the story later to many people, it did not make sense to his listeners. In his words, the first thing he saw was two shiny eyes. As he inched closer, for he was crawling on his belly, he saw vaguely the gray outline of an animal that looked like a very enormous wild boar. Without putting on his hunting lamp he shot and then shot again. There was a loud wail and then a scream—*I am dead*—the wailing voice was Joachim's.

But how could this be? Akwete wondered. When he pointed his gun what he saw was an animal, not a person. He hurriedly carried Joachim in both hands while throwing his gun aside. As he took a few steps out of the forest, Joachim drew his last breath.

Akwete was screaming as he carried his dead friend into town.

"I did not kill him.

"I did not shoot him.

"It was an animal that I shot, not Joachim.

"It was when I moved closer that I saw it was my friend that was bleeding. Please somebody help me."

He was still crying and wailing, his hunting clothes stained with blood, as he cried to the Family House.

Akwete was loved by many but he was also a man with enemies and now they began to talk.

—Was I born today? Who says a human being and an animal have the same shape?—

—He should come up with a more believable story to tell us. He probably killed the man for prosperity rituals—

—He should have thought of a more believable story—

—There has always been something a little not straightforward about that man—

—Instead of following an honest trade like other men, he spends the whole day with other people's wives, cracking jokes with them, smiling with them, touching them and being touched by them and persuading them to go into debt for his colorful fabrics—

But there were also a few people who were on Akwete's side. A few people who knew about hunting said that a hunter who goes into the forest at night to hunt would often encounter quite a few strange things. They talked about animals that lured a hunter deeper and deeper into the forest until the hunter lost his way and ended up being hunted down and devoured by wild animals. They said it was not unusual to encounter animals that were not really animals but people. Evil people transformed themselves into animals to scare hunters. They spoke of birds with melodious voices that sang beautifully in the forest, songs so sweet that hunters dropped their guns and began to listen and listen till they forgot that they were hunters and dozed off for days until they breathed their last and then the bird with the melodious voice descended and pecked out their eyes. They talked of wild boars that had skin so tough no bullet could penetrate them.

—A successful man like Akwete should have been more careful. He has far too many enemies. He is too prosperous for evil eyes not to look in his direction. He has his motorcycle and is said to be planning to build a mansion, why won't evil eyes look at him—

—Remember when every day they offloaded tipper-load after tipper-load of white sand in the place where he was planning to build a house? After which they began offloading cement blocks for days—

—What about the mountains of gravel that were dumped on the same construction site—

—People wondered what kind of mansion he was planning to build—

—You know what they say about a man who spends years and years getting ready to go mad, the preamble for the house construction was like that—

Joachim's family insisted that there was foul play and wanted the full force of the law brought down on Akwete. Akwete ran down to his friend Grandpa.

"See, they want to destroy me. My enemies have finally got me. If I go to jail my business will be all gone by the time I return, that is, if I ever come out of jail alive."

"Panicking will take you nowhere. A man without enemies is an unsuccessful man. The problem is here. The right thing to do is to find a solution to it. You say the family does not want to be paid off. It means they want to make trouble. Nothing can bring back a dead person. But if they want to be unreasonable, there is nothing you can do."

"So do I simply fold my hands and go to prison?"

"Nobody said anything about you going to prison."

"So what is it going to be?"

"Someone will go to prison on your behalf. It has been done before. Whatever sentence is passed on you, that person will serve the jail time. We will ensure that the sentence is short. This is a case of manslaughter, not murder, for indeed Joachim was your friend and you had no plans to kill him, neither have you profited in any way from his death."

"So who will agree to go to jail on my behalf?"

"There are so many people under this roof, we will find somebody. You will reward him highly for serving your time on your behalf. You will marry him a wife. You will build him a house. You will set him up in business when he is released."

"That is not a problem."

It was done.

Uwa was the one who was asked to go to jail on Akwete's behalf. Uwa was the one who was often called upon to carry out any duty that people found impossible to do in the house. He untightened fast screws, he found lost things, he crawled into and out of tight corners, he once jumped into the well to bring out a child that had accidentally fallen in.

Promises were made to him.

"Look, you are young. You still have your best years ahead of you."

"By the time you come out you will live like a rich man for the rest of your days."

"You have nothing to worry about; as I am building my own house I will also be completing one for you. You will move into your own mansion as soon as you are out."

"You will definitely not regret doing this."

"Wives, children, a house of your own, and even a textile business of yours is guaranteed. I will put you in touch with the suppliers, and here's the good thing, you'll not need to peddle and hawk your goods like me. You'll sit gently in your store and all your customers will come to you."

Uwa did not need any convincing. What was his life worth? He could have done it for free.

No one knows for sure how things like this were arranged, but everyone knew that Akwete went on trial and was sentenced but Uwa was the person who went into the prison vehicle and was driven off to jail.

But soon after Uwa's departure for prison, Akwete became a completely different person. He began to drink. Just as he went from place to place trying to sell his clothes in the old days, he now went from one drinking place to another. He was often too drunk to sell his clothes or even to ride his motorcycle home after his drinking bouts.

—It is the spirit of the man he shot. Some people have a really strong spirit that cannot be appeased—

—What is he trying to mask by drinking? There must be something he is hiding from—

—He committed two forms of evil. He killed his friend and should have served the punishment, but, no, he has connections and will not serve his punishment like other people, he hires someone to serve his punishment for him, but look who is being punished now—

—You can run from your atrocities but you surely cannot hide from your atrocities, this is a lesson for all who do evil—

Soon Akwete was owing money to the large textile distributors who had sold him the clothes on credit. He had abandoned the house he was supposed to be building. He began selling off those things that he could still sell off in order to have money to drink.

A few people called him to talk to him about his new lifestyle but he mocked them.

"Don't worry about me. Worry about yourselves. You think my wealth is gone? My wealth that is on the way is going to be one hundred times bigger than whatever I had before. Don't worry yourselves; the same lips laughing at me now will be the same lips that'll praise me in the not too distant time."

By the time Akwete died, which was not long after Uwa had gone to prison, there was nothing of his wealth left. He even owed those whom he had been buying drinks from.

It was a few people who remembered him, especially the women who put money together to give him some kind of burial, befitting or not.

And what about Uwa?

He did the time and came out. He was released far ahead of time for good behavior. Even while in prison, he still put to use his skill for doing what ordinary people found difficult to do.

He was expecting to move into a mansion and be set up in business and to live happily from then on. He heard of the death of Akwete and the burial of his promises.

He returned to the Family House. He was not broken even one bit. To those who asked him how he felt, he had only one response.

"I still have my life, yes, I still have my life," he said to them, moving on to attend to some errand.

I be said I must give the house a befitting name. We all called it the Family House, I said. By what other name should I call it? You must give the house a name that evokes prestige, a name that will make people respect the people who lived in the house and the house itself. So what name do you suggest I call it? You can call the house White Castle of Peace. But it was not white in color, it was not a castle, and it was not that peaceful, I said. You can call it the Grand House on the Hill. You can call it Eagle Terrace. You can call it the Purity Villa. You can call it Peace Haven or Giant Oaks Villa. Give the house a good name because a good name is better than gold, and a man's house is his castle and every man is king in his own abode.

And what about Grandpa and all the things that happened in the house? I asked Ibe. Grandpa was an illustrious and generous man. He fed the poor and the beggars, he clothed the naked and the orphans and widows, he was a man of legendary generosity. He was more generous than Rockefeller. He mounted loudspeakers outside so that people could listen to the music he listened to, he entertained himself and others. He invited the whole street to come and watch television in his house, those who could not find space to sit inside watched through the window screen while some stood by the door, Ibe said.

And what about the woman that was stripped naked and had her head shaved and was paraded around the town? Ibe said the woman was only enacting a ritual drama. A drama? Yes, she was taking part in a traditional ritual for cleansing the community of the sins of everyone. She bore the shame of everyone. What she did for the community was like what Christ did for the whole world.

Are you sure about this? Trust me, I remember everything. She was rewarded richly for her role in that traditional ritual. But she was cursed as she moved through the community, don't you remember? You are the one who does not remember. People beckoned to her to come closer so they could drop some money into the calabash she was carrying on her head.

Do you remember the uncle who told his followers to sell all they had because the world was going to end? Of course, I remember him. He was a true prophet. He heard the voice of God. God actually told him he was going to destroy the earth, but like a good prophet he interceded with God to show a little mercy and give the people a chance to repent. And the people that threatened to burn down the house? Nobody threatened to burn down the house. The people went away rejoicing that their lives had been spared and that the world did not end. They went away singing his praises and calling him a true prophet.

And what about the soldiers who came to . . . ? What soldiers? Oh the soldiers. Grandpa had friends, some of whom were soldiers, officers, engineers, lawyers, policemen. All kinds of professionals came to the house.

And what about Baby? Oh, Baby? No man was willing to marry her but Grandpa was always generous so he found her a husband. He even paid the man to marry her, I think.

And what about all those kids in the house? I told you already that Grandpa was generous and kind and did not allow orphans to suffer so he brought them all under his roof and fed them and sent them to school.

Do you remember any suffering in the house? No one suffered in the house. It was the sound of laughter and the sound of spoons on teeth and the sound of food on its way down to the gullet that people heard coming from the house.

And do you happen to remember that one time that you were sick? Me sick? I have never been sick in my life. I was not sick. I was in a trance. I was seeing the future. I was sitting with God in heaven and he was showing me the future of everybody, including you. You had appendicitis but we thought it was because of the money and other stuff we took from the shrine. You imagine a lot of things, not as they were, but as you want them to be. I was in a trance and I saw God, he was wearing cream-colored trousers that swept the ground and his beard was as white as snow.

HOW THE HOUSE CAME TO BE NO MORE

There were soldiers carrying guns and *koboko* horse whips. There were civilian members of the Environmental Task Force in yellow overalls. There was an engineer in blue overalls and a white safety helmet. There was a policeman on an impatient horse that refused to stand still. There was a top civil servant in the Ministry of the Environment dressed in a four-piece suit and tie under the dull yellow glow of the sun and suffocating heat. There was the operator of the bulldozer and his assistant. There was the bulldozer, yellow in color with a large CATERPILLAR logotype on its side. There was a photographer with a camera.

There was a new governor who had just been sworn in. Who had sworn to make the city a modern city. He said the city was filthy. There were open drains clogged with filth. The once-in-a-month sanitation program was not enough. People simply dug up the filth and dirt in the drains and shoveled them into the street and after a few days heavy rains ensured the dirt ended up right where it had come from. He was going to demolish the houses that blocked the city sewage and drainage system. He was going to ensure street trading was abolished. He wanted houses to have a fresh coat of paint and he insisted on the planting of flowers and palms along the major roads.

The Ministry of the Environment sent a notice that the Family House was sitting on a place that should have a major drain way. He sent his men to put four large *X*s on the four walls of the house. There were whisperings as to whether the Family House would go down or not. Some said that all the juju that lay buried in the house would ensure it didn't fall. Others said that the evil committed in the house was enough to pull the house down.

The morning the bulldozers came, accompanied by members of the newly constituted task force on the environment, no one told them that a former occupant of the house had been a task force member, that he was called Soja and that whatever had killed him was not unconnected with his duties as a member of one other task force a long time ago. Down the street a song boomed from a loudspeaker. The lyrics of the song went this way—*vanity upon vanity, all is vanity*. About half an hour later the track being played would change to another song titled *Oh Merciful God* . . .

There were also the people on the street who had gathered to witness the demolition of this house that had long been abandoned but of which they had heard strange stories.

—But why all the soldiers and policemen and guns and horses? Is it not an ordinary house?—

—That house is no ordinary house. Ordinary house, indeed—

—But it is not as if the house is going to run away. The house has no legs with which to run—

—If you knew all the things that have happened in that house you'd know that it can do more than run—

—People say that at night you could hear voices and sometimes cries emanating from that house. Even though no one lives there anymore—

—It casts a dark shadow on our street. They should demolish it so that light will take over from darkness—

—All the things they said happened in that house before you were born will make your ears tingle—

—But how would you feel if they decide to demolish your own house that you built with your own sweat and blood because the new ruler wants to beautify the city by planting flowers and painting houses—

—That house was built with the sweat of innocent, hardworking people—

—Wait; hold on a minute. What is going on? See, what did I tell you? That is no ordinary house—

The bulldozer was about to sink its teeth into the house when it belched and coughed and sputtered to a stop. It gasped and then its motor stopped running. There was a brief silence and then the horse neighed and made as if it was about to bound off, but it was restrained by the police rider.

"What is wrong?" the leader of the task force, the big boss from the Ministry of the Environment, asked.

The bulldozer operator and his boy jumped down, looking confused. This had never happened before. The bulldozer was almost new and had never stalled.

"Let me check the plugs, maybe they overflowed," he said, and brought out a handkerchief, wiped his face, and began searching for the plugs.

—You see what I told you, they must have buried something in that house—

—You don't do this kind of work if you are not strong. To do this type of work with an *ordinary* hand and with no protection is to court death—

—That is true, though. Even the engineers that construct bridges, white engineers, Germans, Israelis, American engineers, they buy rams sometimes cows or chickens to make sacrifices to the river goddess before they start constructing bridges—

—These ones should know better, they have been doing this job for long. They know that you cannot just demolish a house built by someone just like that—

The bulldozer started working again. This time the driver and the bulldozer went at the house as if doubly determined and soon there was rubble and dust. As a part of the house came down the members of the task force who were standing a little distance away began to clap and cheer. The song playing from the record store came to an end and a new song came on: "My Father's Mansion in the Sky," *In my father's house there are many mansions*, the musician sang as the dust rose like a sacrificial burnt offering from the crumbled Family House into the sky.

ACKNOWLEDGMENTS

I could never have done this alone. Heartfelt thanks to my family: Evelyn, Aisha, Michael, ChuChu, Cheta, CJ.

My agents Jin Auh and Jackie Ko in New York, and Sarah Chalfant and Luke Ingram in the U.K.

My editors Tim Duggan, Emily Cunningham, Bella Lacey, and Michal Shavit.

Oscar Casares, the New Writers Project at the University of Texas–Austin, where I served as a visiting assistant professor in the spring semester of 2013, and where some parts of this book were written.

And to my colleague Eric Bennett, who read an early draft of this book, for his encouraging words.